"*A Planet for Rent* is the English-language debut of Yoss, one of Cuba's most lauded writers of science fiction. Translated by David Frye, these linked stories craft a picture of a dystopian future: Aliens called xenoids have invaded planet Earth, and people are looking to flee the economically and socially bankrupt remains of human civilization. Yoss' smart and entertaining novel tackles themes like prostitution, immigration and political corruption. Ultimately, it serves as an empathetic yet impassioned metaphor for modern-day Cuba, where the struggle for power has complicated every facet of society."

JUAN VIDAL, NPR, BEST BOOKS OF 2015

"In prose that is direct, sarcastic, sexual and often violent, *A Planet for Rent* criticizes Cuban reality in thinly veiled terms. Cuban defectors leave the country not on rafts but on 'unlawful space launches'; prostitutes are 'social workers'; foreigners are 'xenoids'; and Cuba is a 'planet whose inhabitants have stopped believing in the future.' . . . The book is particularly critical of the government-run tourism industry of the '90s, which welcomed and protected tourists—often at the expense of Cubans—and whose legacy can still be felt today."

JONATHAN WOLFE, *THE NEW YORK TIMES*

"Some of the best sci-fi written anywhere since the 1970s. . . . Like its author, a bandanna-wearing, muscle-bound roquero, *A Planet for Rent* is completely sui generis: riotously funny, scathing, perceptive, and yet also heart-wrenchingly compassionate. . . . Instantly appealing."

ANDRÉ NAFFIS-SAHELY, *THE NATION*

"This hilarious and imaginative novel by Cuba's premiere science-fiction writer gets my vote for most overlooked novel of the year. Yoss's book imagines a world where Earth is run as a tourist destination by capitalist aliens who have little regard for the planet or its inhabitants. *A Planet for Rent* is a perfect SF satire for our era of massive inequality and seemingly unchecked environmental destruction."

LINCOLN MICHEL, *VICE*

"*A Planet for Rent* is devastating and hilarious and somehow, amidst all those aliens, deeply human."

DANIEL JOSÉ OLDER, AUTHOR OF *HALF-RESURRECTION BLUES*

"A compelling meditation on modern imperialism. . . . A fascinating kaleidoscope of vignettes. . . . A brilliant exploration of our planet's current social and economic inequities. . . . Yoss doesn't disappoint, sling-shotting us around the world and the galaxy. . . . Striking, detailed. . . . Yoss has written a work of science fiction that speaks to fundamental problems humans deal with every day. This is not just a story about alien oppression; it's the story of our own planet's history and a call for change."

"What *1984* did for surveillance, and *Fahrenheit 451* did for censorship, *A Planet for Rent* does for tourism. . . . It's a wildly imaginative book and one that, while set in the future, has plenty of relevance to the present."

"Cuba has produced an author capable of understanding science fiction by writing it like it's rock and roll. Yoss is a thoughtful author who simply seems to understand his work and science fiction better than many of us."

"Read this if you liked: Stanislaw Lem, William Gibson's Sprawl trilogy. . . . An excellently written piece of sci-fi, with its rich world-building and well-crafted characters. . . . Yoss has told a fictional tale that rings all too true despite the aliens and spaceships. *A Planet for Rent* is science fiction of the highest caliber. It tells us to imagine a strange new world, and as we explore it we come to understand our own a little better."

"[Yoss's] work is modern, dynamic and yet deep and thoughtful. . . . There is a dark, almost bleak tone to the novel but with small sparks of hope, along with a good deal of dark humor. . . . It's wildly inventive, imaginative fiction, with a real edge to the writing—there is an energy to the prose that is almost tangible and to get all this through a translation is nothing short of remarkable."

ANT JONES, SFBOOK.COM, FIVE-STAR REVIEW

"The true power of science fiction lies in its capacity to convey the reality of human existence, and the threats we face from internal and external sources, while using language, images, and concepts that transcend common experience. This could not be truer of *A Planet for Rent* by Cuban science fiction legend José Miguel Sánchez, better known as Yoss. . . . Highly relevant. Joining a literary tradition of writers who envisioned Earth's future in terrifyingly comprehensible ways, such as H.G. Wells, Arthur C. Clarke, J.G. Ballard, Philip K. Dick, Aldous Huxley, and Margaret Atwood, Yoss's portrayal of Earth's dystopian downfall weaves together fantasy and reality—at times troublingly close to the latter. . . . Yoss skillfully weaves themes and characters together into a rich tapestry, and each section gives us a more fulfilling, and fearful, vision of a dominated Earth–now an intergalactic tourist destination."

ROSIE CLARKE, WORDS WITHOUT BORDERS

"Intergalactic space travel meets outrageous, biting satire in *Super Extra Grande*. . . . Its author [Yoss] is one of the most celebrated—and controversial—Cuban writers of science fiction. . . . Reminiscent of Douglas Adams—but even more so, the satire of Rabelais and Swift."

NANCY HIGHTOWER, *THE WASHINGTON POST*

"A lighthearted space-opera adventure by Cuban author Yoss. . . . This novel's madcap tone is very similar to Douglas Adams'—so much so that it's almost impossible to avoid drawing such comparisons (although Adams didn't joke about oral sex with aliens, as Yoss does here). As in Adams' works, the galaxy's species are terrifically alien, sporting six breasts and no teeth or breathing methane instead of oxygen. . . . An exceptionally enjoyable comic tale set in a fully realized, firmly science-fictional universe."

KIRKUS, STARRED REVIEW

"Science fiction is a place where minority authors have brilliantly mixed the possibilities of the future with the sociopolitical problems of their time. Everything from politics and sexism to racism and the silence of the subaltern (the one Gayatri Chakravorty Spivak wrote about) have been explored within the context of a narrative that takes place in a fictional future. Cuban science fiction author Yoss' *Super Extra Grande* does all these things. . . . [Yoss] marries hard science with wild invention and throws that mix into a hilarious, politically and sexually charged universe where all alien races have stopped being unknown to each other. The result is a witty narrative that proves that, when done right, science fiction can be the most entertaining genre even when delivering a message. . . . Spanglish dialogue enriches the narrative and makes it crackle with authenticity. . . . Kudos must be given to translator David Frye for his outstanding work. . . . Besides the space it creates to discuss alternate realities, the best science fiction is that which delivers on the promise of its name, and Yoss pulls it off with flying colors in part thanks to his degree in biology and in part thanks to his fearless approach to creation. . . . Yoss tackles science fiction with the attitude of a rock star, and he has the talent to make even his wildest ideas work. *Super Extra Grande* follows the parodic tradition of Cuban science fiction and treads new grounds in terms of the amount of imagined science and fauna found in its pages. This is a narrative in which anything is possible, love and desire are thrown into the tumultuous new territory of interspecies relationships, and Spanglish is the unifying language of the galaxy. In other words, this is science fiction at its best: wildly imaginative, revolutionary, full of strange creatures, and a lot of fun to read."

GABINO IGLESIAS, *PANK MAGAZINE*

"This newly translated novel by Yoss, considered one of the masters of contemporary Cuban sci-fi, transports us to a bizarre vision of the far future, where humanity has mastered space travel and discovered it is but one small corner of a vast, very strange intergalactic tapestry."

JOEL CUNNINGHAM, BARNES AND NOBLE BEST SCIENCE FICTION & FANTASY OF 2016

"A brawny, gregarious rockero who looks like he just walked off the set of a Van Halen video, circa 1984, Yoss is one of the most visible members of Cuba's small but dynamic sci-fi scene. He is also one of the more prolific writers on the island, having published more than 15 novels and books of short stories, and two books of critical essays, as well as numerous anthologies of science fiction and fantasy short stories. . . . As someone who has made his living as a writer since 1988, when his novel *Timshel* won Cuba's David Prize for first-time authors, he has been a keen observer of Cuban society (and its literature) for almost three decades. . . . Yoss's more recent novel . . . dares us to hope for a universe in which all things (super extra) large and small can find their place."

EMILY MAGUIRE, *LOS ANGELES REVIEW OF BOOKS*

"Get ready to enter the world of the fantastic, phenomenal and downright freaky. If you like huge space monsters, faster-than-light travel, erotic six-breasted aliens with strange reproductive habits, atomic blasts, gastrointestinal diseases

and interplanetary warfare, then this is the book for you. . . .
It sounds crazy doesn't it? And it really is. This book is utterly
unlike any other sci-fi novel you will have read before. . . .
The marvelous thing with writing about the future is you
can really let your imagination run wild and Yoss certainly
decided to take full advantage of this poetic license."

JADE FELL, *ENGINEERING & TECHNOLOGY MAGAZINE*

PRAISE FOR
CONDOMNAUTS

"Yoss (*Super Extra Grande*) is an eminent Cuban SF writer
who also fronts a heavy metal band; his iconoclastic spirit
and rock-and-roll aesthetic are on full ingenious display in
this daring, rollicking, and joyous novel. . . . The novel is
recognizable as a space opera, but everything from human
history to the economics of galactic trade is seen from a
richly irreverent angle. Josué is a three-dimensional, well-
rounded protagonist whose flaws can be genuinely aggra-
vating without overwhelming his natural charm. When
hilarity ensues, as it often does, the laughs are earned and
heartfelt. This extended dirty joke is also an impressive
science fiction novel with much to say about sex, culture,
and what it means to be alien."

PUBLISHERS WEEKLY, STARRED REVIEW

"The book pays off in a climax that a well-trained Condomnaut would be proud of. What I loved about *Condomnauts* isn't just its unusual structure or how Yoss (mostly) avoids the obvious smutty gags, it's how he makes this a story about the marginalized. Those earlier scenes detailing Josué's nightmarish upbringing tie into the book's overall discussion about those who exist outside the mainstream, whether it's because of their color, their class, or their sexuality, and who find themselves, due to a strange set of circumstances, empowered to act. . . . *Condomnauts*, brought brilliantly into life by David Frye's translation, is an unconventional space opera that's heartfelt, brazen, exciting, and just a little bit naughty."

IAN MOND, *LOCUS MAGAZINE*

"In *Condomnauts*, Yoss takes readers to the 24th-century Rubble City, Cuba, where Josué Valdes makes a living racing cockroaches. But he finds his true calling as a sexual adventurer in space, where he serves as an ambassador for the Nu Barsa colony. Yoss is Cuba's preeminent writer of science fiction, and this raucous novel is a fun introduction to the universe he's populated with humans who use sex to seal intergalactic treaties."

LORRAINE BERRY, *SIGNATURE*

"Following the success of *Super Extra Grande* and *A Planet for Rent*, Yoss brings us another uproarious space adventure with *Condomnauts*, a wildly inventive and unapologetic tale that would make even Barbarella blush."

KAYTI BURT, DEN OF GEEK

"A hilarious and a fantastic read. Human sexuality and stereotypes are questioned all while delivering page after page of heart-pounding and belly-laughing fun."

TRACY PALMER, SIGNAL HORIZON

"*Condomnauts* is everything a good space opera should be—far-reaching, glimmering, gut-wrenching, perilous—but stickier. Much, much stickier."

THE ARKANSAS INTERNATIONAL

ALSO BY YOSS

A Planet for Rent
Super Extra Grande
Condomnauts

YOSS

~~RED DUST~~

A NOVEL

Translated from the Spanish by
David Frye

RESTLESS BOOKS
BROOKLYN, NEW YORK

First published as *Polvo rojo* in *Premio UPC 2003*
by Ediciones B, Barcelona, 2004

First Restless Books paperback edition July 2020

Paperback ISBN: 9781632062468
Library of Congress Control Number: 2018956661

This book is supported in part by an award from
the National Endowment for the Arts.

NATIONAL ENDOWMENT for the ARTS
arts.gov

Cover design by Edel Rodriguez
Set in Garibaldi by Tetragon, London

Printed in Canada

1 3 5 7 9 10 8 6 4 2

Restless Books, Inc.
232 3rd Street, Suite A101
Brooklyn, NY 11215

www.restlessbooks.org
publisher@restlessbooks.org

To Raymond.
Chandler, that is.

And to my father,
who asked me for a crime novel years ago. . . .
and waited.

ONE

THIS IS THE STORY of how I got my secondname.

But it's also the story of Vasily, of Old Man Slovoban, of Makrow 34 and Giorgio Weekman, of Zorro, Mao Castro, Achilles, and so many more. Humans, pozzies, aliens. And it's the story of the *Burroughs*, of course.

I wish I could start it like this:

The desert wind was blowing that night, loaded up on red dust like a drunk on whiskey.

Then go on something like this:

It was one of those hot dry Santa Ana winds blasting down through the mountains, curling your hair and making your nerves jump and your skin itch. It was one of those nights that drive people crazy, making men throw punches in every bar and meek wives finger the edge of the butcher knife and study their sleeping husbands' necks. One of those nights that somehow always end in blood and murder.

Suggestive, isn't it? It's my own take, not my own style. I pinched it. My gloss on Raymond Chandler. Twentieth century. Hard-boiled detective fiction. Unfairly forgotten today, but my favorite writer all the same. The guy I chose to honor when it was my turn to pick a keyname.

Would have made a nice opening for the story, don't you think?

Except that's not how it happened.

First off, there was no *burning wind from the desert at night, blasting down through the mountains and driving people crazy.*

Mainly because my bosses, the aliens who run the Galactic Trade Confederation, worship uniformity. It's good for business. Almost as much as they despise unwelcome surprises. The aliens have a saying: *Routine is the mother of efficiency and the grandmother of profit.* When they designed this trading station, the *William S. Burroughs*, they left out all the fun geographic stuff. No deserts, no mountains. The onboard oxygenating gardens spread out over hundreds of square kilometers, all smooth as a tabletop. Not quite a tabletop—smooth as a high-gain parabolic radar-antenna. The inner surface of our little world is concave, you know, not flat. Let's not get on the wrong side of Euclidean geometry.

The aliens who designed this station opted for the plan favored by the ink-slingers who illustrated those old mid-twentieth-century fantasy books, the ones about the conquest of outer space. A giant space wheel.

The aliens already had artificial gravity—they're the ones who let humans in on the secret—so they didn't need to spin the *Burroughs* like a top to make Earthlings feel at home. For them, the shape was nothing functional. Just a hat-tip. Or a sarcastic reminder. That's their style, the big bosses.

There's no real nighttime here, either. Other than the endless night of outer space, I mean. If you ever get so bored you start staring out one of the handful of portholes that the tightfisted designers were negligent enough to build into the structure, what's there to see? Darkness. Maybe Titan, a dreary crescent moon, far off in the distance. Even farther, the enormous bulk of Saturn.

We're parked in a Lagrange point of the Saturn system. If the lighting were any good, it would be a magnificent spectacle. But as far as we are from the sun there's not much light. When the planet's rings and its titanic moon don't block the dim sun, the puny smidgen of daylight that breaks through isn't bright enough to bother a bat.

We have artificial light twenty-four hours a day. Or thirty-six, if you count days like the Colossaurs. Whatever. Point is, the lights never go off. What a waste of energy. Some pozzies who go in for philosophizing, like my pal Zarathustra Heidelberg, say the aliens keep the lights on all the time because you never know when somebody will be awake and closing a deal. Plus, it's good for the plants. But hard-nosed guys like me, we suspect they just do it because they know it bugs the humans. Throws them off their circadian sleep cycles. That alien sense of humor again.

If a Homo sapiens doesn't like the light set-up—they could simply stay home.

As for me and my friends—we never sleep anyway.

But I'm getting ahead of my story.

Since we're on the only station in the Solar System where humans can get a license to rub elbows with aliens and make intergalactic deals, from the human point of view not being here means getting cut out of a very lucrative business. That's what brings Homo sapiens to the premises: trading raw materials from Earth for the sophisticated tech that the Galactic Trade Confederation doles out, sparingly. For all their grumbling and whining, for all the sedatives and painkillers they pop, every human who's brave enough to do the job and anxious to get rich will come to the *Burroughs*, no questions asked. And come back. Again and again.

Here's one more way my story doesn't hold up to my pseudo Chandler: there are no real bars on the *Burroughs*. The bosses like to let the evolved primates of Earth know that they're only guests here, even if there's always at least a couple thousand of them around. No bars that serve drinks a human can stomach, I mean.

No dark rooms full of dames of questionable repute and tough guys whose reputations are not to be questioned, none of the watering holes my favorite writer so lovingly described.

No. Hangouts that sell the sweet sulfur crystals and methanated beverages that Cetians go for—those don't count. No human in his right mind would eat or drink anything so nasty. You can't twist the word *bar* far enough to use it for the cubicles lit like tanning booths where Colossaurs guzzle their thirty kilos of raw meat a day and get all weepy-eyed reminiscing about the bright blue glare of their giant sun. Or the tiny cells where Grodos go to suck their daily ration of vegetable juices, sticking their spiral tongues down into what they call "sophisticated artificial bionutrition systems." To me they look more like big pumpkins with German measles.

If that's not enough, all three alien species who come here prefer to repose in solitude. Must be some weird galactic kink. A bar isn't a bar without a little socialization, is it?

As for meek wives, they've got to be a highly endangered species by now even on Earth itself. But if anybody were to waste their credits bringing one of those rare specimens here, she'd never get near anything so dangerous as a knife. Not by a long shot, at least not while me and my buddies are up and about.

Nobody but a pozzie ever gets past a docking module of the Burroughs bearing arms more dangerous than a pair of nail clippers. A small pair.

Yet even so, there is blood and murder. The first to go were my pals Zorro and Achilles, and the Grodo bounty hunter.

At the time we had no idea it was just the beginning.

TWO

NO MATTER how many times I've watched the holotape, I can't say I was an eyewitness. Not if the word has any meaning. But I was close to the scene. Very close. Cold comfort, considering there was nothing I could do to stop it.

I was on guard duty in Sector 23-A of the docking modules when it all went down. Zorro and Achilles had Sector 24-A, less than an arc-second away. By the time I was on the scene, all I could do was clean up the butchered remains.

Sector 24-A lies between an artificial gravity generator and 25-A, which is permanently offline. It's one of our more isolated sectors. The ship hadn't docked there by accident. The Galactic Trade Confederation had warned us that a couple of bounty hunters, a Grodo and a Colossaur, would be stopping over on the *William S. Burroughs*, almost against their will, to replenish their energy reserves before continuing on their journey.

Seems they were coming from far away. Must have been *very* far away, if they were almost out of fuel—energy crystals are almost inexhaustible. One crystal could have lit my Chandler's old New York City, the whole thing, for a solid decade. The baggers were transporting a prisoner, name of Makrow 34, a fugitive Cetian perp they'd nabbed with no little effort after trailing him for parsec after parsec.

The trading bosses' big blunder was, they forgot to warn us how dangerous this Cetian guy was. Oh, sure, they let us know, in their own half-assed way, that he was a Psi—but they didn't give us any particulars about his exotic talent. Nobody could have seen that coming.

Two days after the fact, when the bureaucrats finally relaxed their security screening and let me peek at his folder, I learned Makrow 34 had started young on a life of crime and had made quite the career of it. Not only had he broken every law in the Cetian, human, and galactic books, he had managed to come up with two or three amusing new crimes of his own.

Amusing for him, not for his victims, I mean.

But that comes later.

The top brass of the Galactic Trade Confederation meanwhile stuck to their compartmentalization policy—*Let not your right tentacle know what your left claw does* would be a good translation of another alien saying. So they didn't see fit to tell us that—what a coincidence—our Makrow 34 had taken advantage of the close resemblance between Cetians and Homo sapiens to commit a good portion of his crimes in our theoretically forbidden Solar System, where he was also suspected of stashing a massive pile of loot. A few thousand terawatt-hours of energy.

One more thing I found out too late.

If my buddies had known, they would have put two and two together and gotten exactly four. One: if the prisoner was working the Solar System, it was a safe bet he had accomplices here. Two: you can always find someone to do the almost impossible in exchange for a few terawatt-hours of energy. Three: if anybody was going to try to rescue him, this station was the only place they could do it. And four: this all added up to big trouble right around the corner.

If they'd known, then Zorro would never have gone to pick him up alone. Precautions would have been taken. Maybe Zorro would have had Achilles with him from the beginning, who knows.

Maybe the two of them would still be around. Maybe not.

Anyway, it wasn't bad judgment that caused Zorro to go there alone. It was lack of information he should have been given. He stuck to standard procedures: one pozzie in the module airlock, another on standby in the dock's outer hatch control room.

Besides, what pozzie—or what Grodo—could have guessed what was about to go down?

I've looped the holotape a thousand times and still can't believe it really happened.

It starts with the usual routine. The airlock hatch opens.

The bounty hunters, like any baggers who've survived long enough in a tough line of work, don't trust each other much and don't like to take risks. The tall, lanky, hexapod figure of the insectoid Grodo and the somewhat shorter but much more massive bulk of the Colossaur, both bristling with weapons (proof that they didn't intend to come in past the docking module) flanked their Cetian prisoner: a tiny humanoid figure, handcuffed and unarmed, almost insignificant in contrast, his profile blurry, as if distorted by some powerful force field.

Like the field that's used to neutralize criminals with the most powerful (and luckily the rarest) Psi powers.

My buddy must have started to suspect something then. You can see on the holotape when he calls Achilles over and starts unbuckling the long whip he always carried under his cape.

At the same moment, a heavy human comes walking calmly around the corner. Zorro pays no attention to him. The fat guy doesn't seem especially threatening. He's coming from the inner zone, where nobody but pozzies have weapons. Most likely he just wandered into the wrong module. Just a matter of warning him off, and—

Zorro never had a chance.

The Grodo must have been caught by surprise, too, when the fat guy suddenly changed direction and went on the attack.

It was fast. Too fast. Any human who moves like that has to be stoked on combat drugs or hyped with military neurocircuit implants. Possession and use of such are strictly off-limits for humans, of course—and not just on the station.

Complicated situation, competing priorities. If the attack had been aimed at any other sort of alien, Zorro wouldn't have skipped a beat before running over to help. He's a pozzie and his mission is to maintain order. But the fat guy went after the Colossaur, so for a second Zorro didn't react even though he already had his whip and sword out, ready for action.

That was his first mistake. A justified one, though. Intervening to help a Colossaur is a deadly insult.

Evolved from predatory reptiloids under a blazing sun, a warrior race par excellence, as devoted to strength and personal bravery as other species are to the arts or technology, the natives of Colossa have taken jobs all over the galaxy as security personnel, soldiers, or guardians (especially now that their planet is at peace, much to their regret). Even the weakest Colossaur would be a thousand times happier to get torn limb from limb than to let some pozzie clown help him tackle a measly human.

It didn't look like he'd need help anyway. A typical Colossaur stands six foot six inches tall and weighs six hundred pounds, and that's not just muscle: a good portion comes from the exoskeleton, a natural bony suit of armor up to two inches thick. The bounty hunter that the fat human attacked was even bigger than normal. A giant among Colossaurs. Nearly ten feet, from his short, thick, muscular tail to the sunken, beady eyes in his armored head. He must have weighed more than nine hundred pounds, and his bony plates were probably three inches thick in places. There's nothing like that on Earth—the closest I can think of is a velociraptor crossed with a giant armadillo.

The people of Colossa aren't the muscle-bound goons they might first appear to be. There's no doubt they rely more on strength than agility, and rightly so: a pozzie, or even a drug-fueled human, could move and react faster. Grodos? Forget about it. Fast as lightning.

Yet even though their fighting methods are based mainly on their incredible power and resistance and their almost absolute lack of weak spots, they aren't the least bit clumsy. On the contrary: they can move with uncanny, lethal fluidity when the situation calls for it, twisting around inside their own shells and taking advantage of the inertia of their own massive bulk, almost like the ancient Japanese sumo wrestlers on Earth.

Considering all this, anyone would have expected the obese human attacker to be reduced to pulp in a fraction of a second. He looked like a baboon trying to go up against a lion, with his hands tied behind his back.

But it turns out the human was very quick. And very fat, too. Fat enough that the impact of his mass, boosted by his onrush, achieved the unthinkable: he knocked the Colossaur down.

The two of them rolled across the floor in a confused heap of bony plates, tail, feet, and scaly or fatty limbs as thick as columns flailing in all directions.

When three more seconds had gone by without the attacker being reduced to ground meat, the Grodo moved so fast that even on the holotape all you see is a blur, rushing over to find out what the fuck had happened to his buddy to keep him from dispatching that insolent, suicidal primate once and for all.

But this time Zorro, true to his duty, did intervene.

That was his second mistake—and his last.

The next instant he was hit squarely by the microwave beam. The mortally wounded pozzie only managed to bring his sword down in a death blow, plunging it up to the hilt in his attacker's side, and there it stayed.

Then Zorro rolled across the floor with what he himself would have called "great style," wrapped in his black cape, letting his velvet Cordovan sombrero fall—and gazing in astonishment, first at the hole nearly a hand wide that had opened up in his stomach, then at the obese human who had made it. Who, by the way, seemed utterly unconcerned with the sharp blade dangling from his torso, and who was still holding the Colossaur bounty hunter's maser.

A maser that, by all rights, should have been individualized. That is: incapable of firing a shot in anyone's hands but its owner's.

Zorro must have left this world full of astonishment.

But he missed one of the best surprises. The Grodo pointed his maser at the pozzie-killer—who should by all the rules of anatomy have been lying on the floor, bleeding out from the sword wound—but the Colossaur fired first. Only he didn't shoot the human. He shot his own astonished companion.

Few energy or projectile weapons in the galaxy (and none that are legal, not even for baggers) can pierce the naturally ultraresistant armor of a Grodo insectoid. Their slick plates make them even slightly more solid than the flashy, impressive armor of the Colossaurs.

But not even a multilayered chitin carapace can save your life when you get hit right in the eye with a jet of acid that penetrates straight to your brain, eating through your flesh.

The Grodo collapsed without a word. Naturally. His race doesn't use words; they communicate with pheromones.

I have to admit, Makrow 34's escape plan was good—half brilliant improvisation, half careful coordination—and it worked to perfection. He'd probably bribed the Colossaur on the way here, promising him part of his energy-crystal booty. But acting alone, even a Colossaur would have been up against impossible odds. Everybody knows a bagger doesn't trust his own shadow, much less another bagger. Old buddies or not.

Plus, it isn't exactly easy to hit a target less than two inches wide, especially not one that can move faster than an express train. Besides, there's also the pozzie.

With his human accomplice pretending to attack him, though, it was almost too easy. In the heat of their phony hand-to-hand combat, it was child's play for the drugged-up human to grab and use the Colossaur's weapon. Especially after the double-dealing bounty hunter had helpfully deactivated the biofield detector that should have kept anyone else from firing it.

With the pozzie suddenly out of the picture, the odds were good that the Grodo would turn all his attention to the killer, freezing for a fraction of a second and making himself a perfect target for a nice acid bath. The Colossaur, slightly slower but outfitted with an ideal Grodo-stopper, needed only to take him out.

Oh, the horrible things greed makes sentient beings do. Treacherously firing on a partner of many years. My Chandler would have written a whole chapter on the immorality of criminals, their lack of principles, something like that.

The holotape time line shows that less than five seconds had passed since the heavy human entered the docking module. Makrow 34, his profile blurry, disarmed inside his anti-Psi force field, had not yet moved.

The dying insectoid bagger wasn't yet done thrashing around on the floor while his nervous system failed, burnt beyond repair by the acid, when the treacherous Colossaur reached down with his thick, scaly arm, and pulled something from his belt. The Cetian's features suddenly became clear, freed from the neutralizing force field. The Cetian smiled and slipped his handcuffs off by simply spreading his arms as if to stretch.

His Colossaur and human accomplices each took a step back. The massive alien's acid-thrower was still dripping. The fat Homo sapiens still had Zorro's sword sticking out of his side, swaying gently, a couple of inches below his left armpit.

Makrow 34 laughed. His laugh, like any Cetian's, was a grotesque parody of human laughter: a grating, disagreeable noise, more lunatic rejoicing than healthy cheer, yet strangely contagious all the same. His two flunkies joined in. The human (identified a second later by the computers as Giorgio Weekman, thief and smuggler of anything that could be smuggled in the asteroid belt) wriggled out of the foamflesh suit that made him look 70 kilos overweight, incidentally serving as a suit of armor to protect him from the Colossaur's blows and Zorro's sword.

A second later Achilles ran in from the control room, firing indiscriminately.

Chastened by Zorro's fate, he'd left his iconic Achaean sword, shield, and lance in the control room, wielding instead a heavy maser, which of course wasn't ancient Greek by any stretch, nor did it match his delicately sculpted bronze breastplate, but it undoubtedly was a more effective weapon for the fight he anticipated.

It didn't seem to be the home team's lucky day. Moving at a strangely slow pace, Achilles inexplicably missed his first shot. Instead of vaporizing the Colossaur's thick skull (which dodged the shot at a speed his former Grodo companion would have envied), his high-powered microwave beam sliced halfway through a titanium girder a foot above his head. Pushing his quickest reflexes, undaunted, my pozzie friend fired again, almost point-blank.

This time, his maser beam didn't even flare. Still moving in slow motion, as if it was all he could do to react, he couldn't even cover himself. A second later, a shot from an ultrapowered weapon similar to the Colossaur's cut him in half, with a great splattering of bronze droplets from his breastplate, half melted by the tremendous heat wave.

With no one in the command room to stop them, Makrow and his two liberator-sidekicks turned without another look at the pozzies' scattered remains and calmly strolled out through the airlock hatch. Then, after deactivating the tracking device in the bounty hunter ship, they took off, destination unknown, with no one to go after them.

I imagine this was the first time the aliens regretted their excessive prudence. Which was responsible, among other things, for never supplying us, the official keepers of order on board the *Burroughs*, with any sort of armed, rapid patrol ship.

THREE

AT THIS POINT in the story I think it's about time for me to introduce myself and clarify a few points about our station, about us pozzies, and especially about the relationship between our alien bosses and humans in the twenty-second century.

I'm a police officer on board the space station *William S. Burroughs*, the Galactic Trade Confederation's enclave in the Solar System. My keyname is Raymond (as in Chandler, as I may have mentioned). My serial number is MSX-3482-GZ.

Naturally, I'm a pozzie too. In other words, not a human being but one of those *robotic abominations*, the *blasphemous entities, neither alive nor dead*, vilified daily by the unregenerate terrestrial preachers who still think everything was better before the aliens came along. A servant of the devils, as many humans still call the Grodos, Colossaurs, and Cetians, without distinction.

Even though I owe them my very existence, I'm not going to say my employers are exactly angels. Beings interested only in profit must necessarily have a pretty unangelic nature. Still, they aren't all that terrible, either, in my opinion.

But haven't they refused to hand any of their greatest scientific and technological discoveries—hyperspace travel, artificial intelligence, immortality serum, self-induced regeneration, stuff like that—over to Earthlings, even though they easily could? Well, true. By the same token, they haven't exterminated or enslaved humanity, which they could also do. And they've at least maintained trade relations with Homo sapiens. Under their own rules, of course.

Rules they've made absolutely clear. They see humanity as an "unpredictable species." Which is a polite way of saying humans are a stupid and very dangerous race who have to be kept in check. Accordingly, they've shared a few of their secrets with the humans, such as artificial gravity and their universal energy crystals. But that's it. Trade is one thing, promiscuity's another. Partners, not equals. Everyone in their own place. No aliens on Earth, no humans among the stars.

There was a call for a no-man's land, a trading post, and that's why they built the *William S. Burroughs*, this enormous station orbiting around Titan.

The orbit of Saturn's satellite proved perfect: close enough to Earth and its colonies on Mars and the asteroids for slow, plasma-powered human ships laden with grain, petroleum, and art productions to reach it after a couple months' flying time, then get back after two more months loaded with a few universal energy crystals, high-tech materials, and cybernetic control systems. Also conveniently near the system's hyperspace portal (merely a common geometric point half an AU above the plane of the ecliptic, with no immediate identifying signs—no romantic vortices of matter and energy glowing in a thousand colors) but far enough from the rest of the galaxy that, without hyperspace travel (which the aliens have no intention of ever allowing humans to get—not until humans have something valuable enough to trade for it, that is), the stars will remain an unreachable dream for mankind. And a safely uncharted paradise for those stars' own powerful and greedy inhabitants.

There's only one reason why my buddies and I exist: somebody has to enforce the law. Or keep up the appearance of lawfulness, at least, in this no-man's land. We're the only ones authorized to bear arms here—and to use them. We're the customs officers of this borderland between Earth and the Galaxy, the Charons of this River Styx between underdevelopment and high tech.

Waxing poetic, am I? What a pity the reality turns out to be so prosaic. That's a fact. Isaac Asimov proved prophetic with his R. Daneel Olivaw, after all: like him, we pozzies aren't human police officers, just positronic robots. Sometimes reality makes literature look small, even science fiction.

True, ever since the aliens showed up nobody on Earth writes SF anymore. Too bad. I really liked the good doctor's stories. After Chandler, I mean. Maybe now that the future has caught up with humans and it turns out they don't like it, they find it hard to think up new possible tomorrows.

Of course, we're neither dead nor alive, neither earthlings nor galaxians, humans nor aliens, but rather both things— and something more. Or something less.

Earth probably would have preferred a police force consisting of human beings, or of living beings at least, but the Galactic Trade Confederation isn't made up of a single race of aliens. They don't trust humans, but they have just as little faith in each other. Following what by now is an ancient tradition, the police forces of the various Stations (and I'd love to know how many there are; of course, like all interesting facts, that's classified and above a simple pozzie's pay grade) are made up of beings like us.

Neither fish nor fowl. Perfectly fair and neutral. In theory, at least.

Sometimes I wonder what my equivalents on other Stations look like. Quadrupeds? Gas clouds? Do they swim or float in superdense atmospheres? Most likely I'll never find out. But I'm sure they must be very different, at least in appearance. The Confederation sticks to a prudent policy of making their police in each system look like the predominant sentient race there—at least approximately.

That's why we're bipedal, have five-fingered hands with opposable thumbs, our pupils turn in our eye sockets, our jaws move when we speak (using thoracic air compressors, because we don't need to breathe and have no lungs). We even wear clothes even though we have no need for them, strictly speaking. We've got nothing to hide—no genitals, inside or out.

And there are other differences. Though we have tongues in our mouths and noses on our faces, we don't have a sense of taste or smell. And why should we? Well, considering that we work as bloodhounds, a sense of smell might have come in handy. But some paranoid Grodo must have figured that over time we could maybe decipher their pheromonic speech, so smell was out. We don't need to eat or sleep (our teeth and lips are for purely cosmetic purposes), don't sweat or defecate, we have no body hair (except on our heads, some of us; not me), our pseudoskin is red, blue, silver, gold, or any other humanly impossible color (apparently somebody wanted us to look like mannequins), most of our "brains" are in our torsos, not our heads (that's why Weekman, Makrow 34's human henchman, shot Zorro at stomach-level: destroying that region is the most effective way of neutralizing a pozzie; I'm still wondering how he knew), and other such details. It's just a matter of *looking* human—a very different proposition from *being* human.

We're also stronger and faster than humans—but without overdoing it. Yes, our reflexes and strength are superior to the average human's. But our reaction time is slower than a Grodo's and our muscles are weaker than a Colossaur's, for example. (The aliens hate taking risks; they'd never accept a police force of robots that were too powerful for them to beat one-on-one.) That's as far as our superpowers go. We can't fly and don't shoot death rays (at least not without antigrav belts or energy weapons). Much less do we have Psi abilities.

The material part of us, our bodies, are 100 percent human tech: we are manufactured on Earth, Mars, or the asteroids. We have state-of-the-art cybernetic bodies, just like all the industrial robots used in terrestrial factories, except ours are completely android—that is, much more anthropomorphic than any industrial use would require.

Nor are our germanium-foam positronic brains fundamentally different from the computers that guide any terrestrial interplanetary ship.

What makes us special are our—can I say "personalities"? I don't know if the aliens left them up to randomness generators or planned them one by one. The fact is, no two are alike. But as individualized as we are, we still have our limits. Oh, yes, it remains an enigma to human cybernetics how positrons move through our germanium-foam labyrinths; the sole yet definitive alien contribution to the package. The divine spark that animated our dead metallic clay. The thing that turned us into individual entities, with characters, skills, and tastes all our own.

Take our keynames, for instance. They're not just a way of distinguishing us at a glance; they are expressions of our individuality that sometimes extend even to our appearance. As a fan of crime novels and especially those of Raymond Chandler, I always wear a trench coat and a broad-brimmed hat like Humphrey Bogart's. Like Philip Marlowe must have worn. Zorro wore a Cordovan sombrero, a mask, and a black cape to go with his sword and whip. Achilles had his plumed helmet, breastplate, greaves, lance, and shield. Arnold Stallone wears a leather jacket with rivets and dark glasses, after the Terminator. Mao Castro never takes off his khaki Red Guard uniform from Cultural Revolution times. And so on, all of us. It isn't as boring and monotonous as uniforms would be (not that some aliens wouldn't prefer that), but it serves almost the same function: anywhere in the station, if you run into a humanoid who looks like he's stayed up late at a costume party, there's no question, he's one of us.

We pozzies are very democratic. No vertical military structures for us. We don't have ranks. When one of us shows himself to be particularly skillful, judicial, and trustworthy, he's given the honor of choosing a secondname. I suppose it's a trivial thing and doesn't make any difference, but I've always wanted one.

Why should I want anything more?

But our positronic brains are as far as our kinship goes with our virtual predecessors, the Good Doctor's literary creations. No *Three Laws of Robotics* for us. Especially nothing about protecting humans at any cost. We have free will. We get bored, we have fun, some of us even fall in love (it's never happened to me; I think it's an aberrant sado-maso absurdity—as I've mentioned, we have no sex organs—and anyway, not many pozzies go for a female key-identity: the macho police tradition is hard to escape, I guess). There even was a Chacumbele who killed himself, and a George III who went mad.

It all comes with the job. We're pretty stable, psychologically speaking. Anyway, as we like to say: maybe our lives and our intelligence are artificial, but our existence, our feelings, and our problems are completely real.

With computers for brains, our memories never fail us. We can mentally calculate 329 to the nth in an instant, whatever good that does us. What makes us special isn't the number of calculations per second we can perform; it's that, as true living beings, we can function in analogical mode, not logically alone. Make deductions based on insufficient data, self-induce flexible rules of conduct in ourselves, and so on.

Not belonging to any side, we should supposedly be fair and impartial judges and executioners. But even though we couldn't be what we are without the aliens' cybernetic technology, we all feel much closer to human beings than to our "cerebral parents." Maybe it's because we have free access to all of human history, psychology, and art, whereas we can only access similar data from the three alien races when they deem it useful.

Which is almost never.

Who are we, where did we come from, where are we going? That's no problem for us. It's good to know the answer to what humans call the universal questions. We are police officers, we must maintain order, we're happy when we succeed; if the brain circuitry in our torsos gets destroyed we disappear, leaving only a memory of us—that's the whole meaning of our lives. The only deep question I sometimes ponder is: What am I? Do I owe this unique, inimitable Raymond, so different from Ivan Stalin or Miyamoto, which I so enjoy being, entirely to the aliens' detailed programming? Or does free will—or something else—really exist?

I don't know if I'll ever find the answer. I don't know if there is an answer.

In any case, even in the middle of our most abstruse philosophical musings we never forget that the aliens are the ones who are in control. Tough luck to any police officer who does forget. There's only one punishment and one fear for us: a personality wipe. Our bosses have only resorted to this *ultima ratio regum* once. The other stuff they do, like changing our postings or temporarily suspending us, are just administrative measures.

Meanwhile, so long as our brain casings are intact, we're immortal. Though sometimes we have to have a new limb or system installed.

If there's anything we run short of on the *Burroughs*, it's replacement parts.

I wonder what Zorro and Achilles must have thought when they felt the impact of the microwave beam. When they realized they were about to disappear.

If they had time to think anything at all, that is.

FOUR

ANYWAY. Getting back to the story.

Or the chaos. The *Burroughs* was buzzing like a hornet's nest after a brat throws a rock at it.

Of course it was. An alien, dead. An alien from one of the powerful, respected races. A Grodo, no less. (His phero-monal name, translated into Standard Anglo-Hispano, would be something like *Vigilante Fixer of Alien Carroña Who Is Never Taken por Sorpresa*, though the events of the day proved that moniker to be . . . inadequate.) The entire insectoid community was in an uproar, demanding that the responsible parties pay in blood or lymph or brake fluid, they didn't care which, so long as they paid it all, immediately.

Turns out none of the perps stuck around to let the Colossaurs tear them to shreds, or the Cetians mutilate them, or the Grodos turn them into living incubators for their cute carnivorous larvae—quaint custom, that. Makrow 34, Giorgio Weekman, and the Colossaur (we never did get an ID on him; the brass from Colossa aren't keen on divulging data about their people) had taken off for parts unknown, leaving the challenge of tracking, locating, and neutralizing them to the pozzies, and in particular to yours truly.

The Galactic Trade Confederation called an urgent Special Summit. I didn't get to go, of course—none of us pozzies did—but I have a pretty good idea of how it went down: the Grodos waved those six ugly appendages of theirs around and threatened everybody in sight with their ovipositor stings, blaming it all on the Colossaurs. The giant reptiles of Colossa grated their teeth and shook their tails menacingly, insisting the perpetrator was just a renegade and there was no call for blaming their whole species. The Cetians expressed dismay over the outrages committed by the flawed and wayward Cetian while considering how best to screw over the two other races. All this under a very thin veil of politeness.

Realpolitik, in a word.

Somebody had to pay the piper, so it ended in the usual shakedown, just as you'd expect. Either all the criminals got caught, or all the aliens left the Solar System. That would mean the end of human intergalactic trade, sending Homo sapiens back to the technological Middle Ages. They gave this good news to us pozzies to pass along to the humans, seeing as how we were the middlemen, so to speak.

It was a huge mess, and it dawned on us that we might be facing a much more complicated business than a simple gunfight. We all felt sorry that Zorro and Achilles were no longer among us, of course: we may be artificial, but our esprit de corps is real.

Not like it would be any skin off our backs if the humans were deprived of alien trade goods and trash, sentimental considerations aside. But with the aliens gone, there'd be no more reason to keep the *Burroughs* in orbit. They'd decommission it and sell it for scrap—and us along with it, no doubt.

Some pozzies profess a faith in an electronic great beyond and positronic reincarnation, but I doubt they would want to test the hypothesis.

Not within a humanly measurable time frame, I mean.

Faced with this threat, the Positronic Police Force went to Code Red. We had to nab the perps, no matter what. That didn't mean we should all leave the station, though. Business had to keep moving, the show must go on. All it meant was, *for this one time and only as an exception*, somebody had to leave the safety of the *Burroughs* and hoof it across the Solar System, hunting down the fugitives.

As the first officer to reach the scene of the crime, my pals elected me to do the job. The top Confederation brass all agreed.

I accepted. I wasn't particularly keen to go, but somebody had to do their dirty work, right? And if the guys with the secondnames had decided that I was the one for the job, well, maybe this would be my chance to get me a secondname of my own, after it was all over.

Not that they gave me any choice.

They granted me full authority inside the Station—for all the good that would do me. Fortunately, the aliens aren't dumb: seeing as the fugitives must have holed up in some rocky corner of the Solar System, they made a couple calls and got my carte blanche extended over almost all the space under human control. Except Earth, naturally.

Not because the Homo sapiens police didn't want to suck up to our omnipotent employers, but because there's a limit to everything. Too many resentful, xenophobic fundamentalist hotheads on the old planet would give their right arms (not much of a sacrifice, considering the current state of medicine and reconstructive grafts, but take it as a metaphor) to shred one of the hated pozzies, the aliens' guard dogs. Even if I left my usual Humphrey Bogart fedora and trench coat behind, my golden epidermis would give me away. Not even the police could protect me from a determined attacker. Or protect the attacker from my counterattacks. No point stirring things up. I'd get to see Earth some other occasion. There'd be time.

But apart from the sacred cradle of humanity, I could go wherever I wanted. And request (that is, demand) the cooperation of any human authorities, federal or local.

When the Galactic Trade Confederation informed me of the wide authorization I'd been granted, I understood just how worried they were about what Makrow 34 and his friends might do—and that if I didn't find them in time, I'd probably envy the fate of Zorro and Achilles.

First thing I did was rewatch the holotapes, over and over. I was intrigued by what happened to Achilles. He didn't have time to understand what he had run up against, and the first few times I watched the recording, I didn't get it either. It seemed like just a lot of bad luck, all coming at once and at the worst possible time. First he moved too slow and aimed badly. Then more slowness, topped off by a weapon malfunction. We checked, cleaned, and adjusted our weapons every day, so a misfire was unlikely, but it wasn't out of the question.

I started by inspecting my buddy's maser. It was in perfect condition: he hadn't forgotten to oil it, the energy crystals were in top shape, no dust on the prisms. So what, then? Was it the buttered toast phenomenon—always falls butter-side down? Or Murphy's law: whatever can go wrong will go wrong, especially when it does the most harm?

In principle, I don't believe the universe has a statistical grudge against anybody. I kept looking. But it wasn't until I was watching the scene for the third time that I noticed the detail. If I had involuntary muscle reactions like humans do, I would have trembled when I recognized the concentration on Makrow 34's face as Achilles approached him and opened fire.

Especially with Zorro's whip and black sombrero levitating as though the artificial gravity had gone out over that square yard of space. They were in the background, behind him, but perfectly visible.

It could only mean one thing: probabilistic fluctuation.

In other words, our Cetian really was a Psi. Not a telepath, though. Nothing that simple. Achilles' mind, like all our minds, wasn't susceptible to Psi control. He wasn't a teleporter, either, or even a telekinetic; neither of those talents would have given him the time to modify the trajectory of a beam moving at relativistic speeds, such as microwaves.

I know what two and two make. With the impossible eliminated, only the improbable remained.

Makrow 34 had to be a Gaussical.

Gaussical. The term had only entered the human vocabulary (and therefore our own) fifteen years earlier. That was when a Grodo with this unforeseen power—Psi specialists on Earth had never predicted it—thought a Cetian trader had double-crossed him. In one of the internal passageways on board the *Burroughs*, the guy lost the self-control Grodos always show and unleashed a chaos of physical improbabilities. Objects floated in midair. It snowed upwards. Some people even claimed they saw a galloping herd of centaurs. Two-headed centaurs.

As Sandokan Mompracem, the pozzie who's our current expert on alien languages, explained it to me, "Gaussical" is an unhappy effort on the part of a machine translator to turn a highly complicated Grodo pheromonal term into Standard Anglo-Hispano. A more precise translation would come out more like *The Desconsiderado Who Willfully Distorts the Curva de Probabilidades*. Earthlings call it a probability curve, a bell curve, or a Gauss distribution. The machine offered a bunch of possible translations, as it does when it comes up against new concepts. The one that stuck was Gaussical.

I went over the other options once, purely out of curiosity. Two of the most reasonable were *Bellringer-Vándalo* and *Inconsciente-Twister*. Doesn't surprise me Gaussical was the one they went for. At least it gives you an idea of what it's about. And reminds you that spoken languages are sometimes woefully incapable of expressing certain concepts.

I felt great now. Oh yes. So the fugitive was one of those statistically near-impossible Psi oddballs who could alter, through some as-yet undiscovered means, the shape of the Gaussian bell curve that describes the statistical probability of any number of events. The macroscopic equivalent of Maxwell's famous demon, according to a pozzie named Einstein who knows more about physics than Sandokan Mompracem does about alien languages and customs.

Which did nothing to clear things up for me. Then Einstein put it in clear, pedestrian terms: the guy could make it rain inside a closed room. He could generate errors in a computer processor. He could make the molecules in one body momentarily intangible to another body. Fortunately

37

the Uncertainty Principle is universal, so even a Psi case like that couldn't decide beforehand which of all the possible fluctuation effects would occur in any given instance. In the rare cases when a Psi might be able to concentrate hard enough to produce a more controlled, voluntary effect, the Law of the Conservation of Energy says that other completely random events would have to occur simultaneously. Like the gravity-free microzone where my poor pal Zorro's whip and sombrero floated up in the air.

So that's why the aliens were so worried.

The case of Makrow 34 would have given Heisenberg himself a giant headache if he'd had to explain it. Or maybe the strange power was so strong in him, he could laugh at the laws of physics.

The prisoner didn't need to carry weapons. He was a lethal weapon himself. The Colossaur and the human did well to free him as soon as they could. Nobody in his right mind fights by hand if he can get hold of a good maser. Taking on Zorro and the Grodo was the most those two could manage, and that only because they were caught by surprise. On their own, they could never have outfought a well-armed and alert positronic robot. But when the freak started messing with the odds, it was a different story.

Achilles never had a chance. It was a mercy he died without understanding what hit him. First his maser missed, then it stopped working; it could just as easily have exploded or turned into a block of ice—an unlikely but theoretically possible thermodynamic event. Something, in any case, would have happened to keep him from hurting Makrow. The fact is, all the statistical fluctuations of Heisenbergian hell were arrayed against Achilles. He never could have truly harmed the Cetian.

When I really leaned on them, the alien merchants confirmed my suspicions. And, of course, they apologized for not giving us the information sooner. But criminal or not, Makrow 34 was one of them, so the contents of his file had been classified. Go figure.

Now, as the case officer, I had permission to review his file. If I needed to know any other details, I could count on their sincere and complete cooperation. So long as I requested them far enough ahead of time and went through the proper channels and blah blah blah.

Understood?

Yep. Totally. I understood too well. Carte blanche in the Solar System or no, I wouldn't have anything remotely like free access to information. They'd give me all the authority I needed, but they wouldn't tell me anything I hadn't already found out on my own. So not only did I have to find a needle in a haystack, blindfolded, I had to grab it and pocket it—knowing that if I tried the needle might stab me, the hay might burst into flames, a roof beam might fall onto my head, I might be charged by a bull that hadn't been there a second before, or I might be turned into a frog in the blink of an eye.

So what if the frog I'd be turned into would be a positronic robot frog. I still had to try.

At least there was one bit of hope amid all the tragedy: the records of the docking module energy sensors showed that the fugitives' fuel reserves were almost empty, and they hadn't had time to refill them. The two or three crystals they had left wouldn't be enough for even one hyperspace jump. They have to go to some hideout, somewhere in our own Solar System. Probably in the asteroid belt. Makrow 34 was familiar with it and his rumored energy treasure would be waiting for him there. Somewhere. That's where I'd have to go to find them. It would be a matter of time. A matter of combing through all the asteroids, one by one.

Simple, right? The sort of fun I enjoy on weekends. I sent out an order—low priority—to every human police frigate, telling them to let me know if they saw anything out of the ordinary. Given the fugitive's exotic Psi capability, though, I figured they wouldn't find so much as the shadow of his ship. And I was right about that.

Want something done right, you've got to do it yourself. As I said, it was up to me to find the needle in the haystack.

Anybody would have thought my hunt was doomed to fail. If Makrow's treasure was what they said it was, as soon as the outlaws reached it they'd have more than enough energy to beat it from the Solar System and take three spins around the galaxy before I could find them.

But fortunately for me, that sort of childish logic doesn't work for space, gravity fields, and especially the bizarre geography of hyperspace.

Get near the hyperspace jump-off point, you're automatically in the zone that the *Burroughs* detectors sweep. If their ship tried, they'd set off every alarm in the station. Plus a barrage or two of antimatter-headed missiles. I prayed to all the gods I don't believe in that Makrow and his sidekicks would risk it. That would have made the endgame easier. Getting themselves disintegrated would have saved me so many hassles.

Likewise, if by some impossible means (Gaussical means, that is) they managed to escape the radar installations, well, once that monster left our jurisdiction, his adventures would be somebody else's responsibility, you know.

In cases like this, I always ask myself what Philip Marlowe would do, but on this occasion it did me no good. After rereading the complete works of Chandler for the millionth time, I gave up. From what I could tell, there were no Gaussicals on Earth in the 1940s, no aliens, no hyperspace jump-off points in the Oort Cloud, no potential hideouts the size of an asteroid belt where a criminal could lie low.

Or rather—all those things did exist, but they didn't count for anything in the game of hide-and-seek. As for the bad guys' weapons, Marlowe and company had also had it pretty easy in Los Angeles compared to me. What's a lead-filled blackjack and a couple of revolvers next to having all the laws of probability turned against you?

My buddies offered me all the help they could. It wasn't much. They didn't have any suggestions either. My best friend, Chester Spillane, even loaned me his collection of Mike Hammer novels and twentieth-century detective movies, in case I could find any inspiration in them.

I read and watched them all. Good thing I was so meticulous. And lucky for me, my friend had such a wide definition that his detective holotapes included a bunch of cop comedies, restored from old celluloid prints.

48 Hours. Leads: Nick Nolte and Eddie Murphy. Archetypes, almost caricatures. The simple, slightly brutish but honest white policeman. The clever, sardonic black criminal (small-time criminal, of course, so viewers could identify with him: bad, but not that bad). Not much in the way of research, though pretty entertaining. The thing is, it made an idea bubble up through my germanium-foam circuits.

Why not follow the white cop's lead? Fight fire with fire. Use a bad guy to trap another bad guy.

Homeopathy. Like seeks like.

Since the *Burroughs* obviously didn't keep any Cetian smugglers, murderers, thieves, or swindlers on hand, it was logical and completely inevitable that, after a quick trip to the station's nanoelectronic workshops, half an hour later I'd be walking into the force-field cell for my first meeting with Vasily Fernández.

FIVE

I HAD READ HIS FILE. It clearly said what he was: a little guy with no relevant qualities. That's all he was, at first sight. A high-security cell isn't the best place for bulking up on steroids, installing a super-cyborg arm, or getting plastic surgery. He still was more skinny than stout, more short than tall, just another Slavic-Latino, ordinary face, average intelligence.

But did I say *no relevant qualities*? Sorry, my mistake.

A minor detail. Almost nothing. The statistical genetic lottery has also cursed him with the strongest, most uncontrollable, least comprehensible, least desirable Psi gift of them all.

You guessed it. Vasily Fernández was the only other known Gaussical. Not counting that first furious Grodo,

I mean. He was also the only Gaussical born on Earth in the past 150 years. That is, since the aliens made contact with the human species. If there were others before him (I suspect that Alexander the Great and Napoleon Bonaparte may have been Gaussicals, for example, but I can't prove it), they probably had the same experience he did at first: they had no idea what they were.

Orphaned so young he never knew his parents, after leaving the charity orphanage Vasily began to make his way as a purse-snatcher, pickpocket, small-time thief, forger, and two-bit flimflammer. And he seemed to be doing a decent job of it. His hard work earned him a nickname, *El Afortunado*, for his incredible luck.

But his career took a wrong turn when he finally realized that what he was getting away with couldn't be a simple matter of good luck—or bad luck for everybody else. Having access to information supposedly off-limits to Homo sapiens (one of these days the aliens are going to have to get serious about the dark Web), he connected the dots and realized he was a living unlikelihood, a Gaussical. That made him cocky, ambitious; he figured there was no chance he'd ever get caught. He was right about that for several months. So long as he stuck to Earth, Mars, and the asteroids.

But when he tried expanding his operations to the *Burroughs*, for reasons he never spilled, it only took my buddies five days to detect and catch him. I admit it wasn't easy. Vasily worked alone, he was slippery and cautious, and while his weird abilities never came close to the controlled power that Makrow 34 displayed in his escape, my buddies Ivan and Miyamoto suffered a few setbacks during the investigation that they put down to bad luck—until it occurred to them to add an anti-Psi force field to their "hunting gear." That was the end of the strange happenings. Soon they netted their fish, and then Vasily El Afortunado's forays came to a stop. After that, Ivan was no longer just Ivan; he became Ivan Stalin.

But even as he fell, El Afortunado somehow managed to land on his feet. His track record and psychological profile showed that he wasn't a deviant or a sociopath. In plain words, not such a bad guy. He just didn't know a better way to make a living than by dodging the law. He hadn't committed any serious crimes on Earth, Mars, or the asteroids, and hadn't caused significant damage. On our station he simply hadn't had time to do much. So he avoided the death penalty usually meted out to wanton Psis and only got ten years in prison.

He'd done three of them right here on the *Burroughs*, of course. Anywhere else in the Solar System would have been unthinkable. The aliens wouldn't have allowed humans to access the necessary Psi-proof force-field technology in a thousand years. So it was either keep him here, let him go, or kill him. The humans never would have accepted the second option, and the aliens refused to consider the third, so here he stayed.

A good thing, too. Their paranoid precaution would now give a huge boost to me, the Galactic Trade Confederation, and—if he treated me straight—maybe even Vasily himself.

"I got nothing to tell nobody they ain't already dragged out of me a hundred times with their damn drugs, and I ain't interested in the shitty benefits of any fucking rehab program," he politely informed me by way of greeting when I stepped into his cell. "Maybe they made me a snitch against my will, but they won't make me a bootlicker for the aliens like you guys. Come on, pozzie, you look ridiculous in that B-movie detective get-up," he went on. "Who do you think you are, Dick Tracy?"

I activated the compressor pumps in my chest and sighed. It sounded exactly the way I wanted: melodramatically impressive. The truth is I was worried, though. Did he know as much about twentieth-century crime fiction as he seemed to?

I'd have to tread carefully. I'd already figured out from his file that he'd be a hard nut to crack. He was a perfect example of a person convinced that, if the world had had enough of him, he'd had enough of the world. He was kind of right about that, from his point of view: he didn't have anyone or anything waiting for him on the outside.

But I had to get him on my side. I didn't have any choice, if I wanted to catch Makrow 34 before he screwed over the entire Solar System. Only one choice for him, and it had to be yes.

I took off my fedora, like I was getting ready for a long, sincere conversation, and pulled what looked like a super-sophisticated wristwatch from a trench coat pocket to show him. "My name is Raymond, Vasily, and I'm here to make you an offer you can't refuse—not unless you're a complete idiot. Know what this is?"

It was a rhetorical question, of course, but he couldn't keep his mouth shut. "I suppose it's your videophone-balls-cratcher-wristwatch, Dick Tracy," he growled, and I felt a little better. My trick had worked: at least now I knew he'd never seen *The Godfather*. If that was true, and the gods were smiling on me, maybe he hadn't watched *48 Hours* either. It seemed he was just a fan of the yellow-hatted cop in the funny pages.

"Wrong. It's a portable anti-Psi field generator. Pure nanotech, an experimental prototype, courtesy of our good friends from the Galactic Trade Confederation. Don't let the shape fool you. You wear it around your neck, not your wrist."

He shrugged, a perfect show of not giving a damn, but I caught a dim spark of interest deep in his green eyes. He'd taken the bait! Now all I had to do was reel him in slowly, carefully, and I'd have him.

"So," I went on, feeling more and more sure of myself. "Want to know what it does? It goes around a Psi criminal's neck, and whenever he's about to use his ability, this little baby activates and stops him. It doesn't have to stay on all the time—a real energy-saver. Sweet invention, isn't it?" A sly grin came across Vasily's face. It didn't take Psi powers to guess what he was thinking. "Oh, I almost forgot. Some paranoid sadist who's allergic to trusting other people's good intentions decided at the last minute to add a little explosive capsule to the design. A precisely calculated quantity of Ultrasemtex. There's no risk it might blow up by accident from getting bumped or what have you, but if somebody tries taking it off and ditching it—boom!" I luxuriated in the explosive onomatopoeia. "The guy ends up minus a head, and nobody around him gets a scratch. That's why we don't put it on your wrist or ankle—some people wouldn't mind trading a limb for freedom. Especially with all the regeneration tech they have these days, it's not like losing a hand is forever. But even a Grodo can't live long without a head."

"Neat toy," Vasily allowed. "But what's it to me? I ain't no fucking alien lover."

We'd have to do something about his language.

"This interesting little device represents your conditional freedom," I said, and tossed it into his lap, casual. "The decision is yours. If you agree to wear it and give me some help, you won't have to spend the next seven years of your sentence in this little box. Well, let's call it six years, because they tell me your behavior has been exemplary. They'll knock a few months off, count on it."

El Ex-Afortunado lifted his hands—then stopped, halfway to his neck. "I knew it was a trick. Pozzies never play square." He dropped the collar like a kid who's tired of a toy and pushed it my way with one foot, scornful. "Might as well leave, pozzie. I'm doing okay here. I got room to exercise, I got enough books to read and enough tapes to watch to last me three lifetimes, all the virtual sex I could want, and—"

"And nobody to share it with and nobody to talk to. No streets, no freedom, no real life." I cut him short, triumphant, and picked up the collar without offering it to him a second time. "So don't tell me you're not interested, because I'm not going to believe you."

"Hmm, maybe," he admitted, reluctantly. "Come on and spit it out, pig. Tell me what you want from me. You gotta have something pretty heavy on your hands or you wouldn't be taking a chance with a superdangerous Gaussical like me."

I didn't set him straight about how dangerous he was—not yet. I told him the whole story in broad strokes, even about the stash of energy crystals that Makrow 34 might have hidden somewhere in the asteroid belt.

When I was done, Vasily let out a short but infectiously lighthearted laugh.

"I get it. Cute little assignment your bosses dumped on you, pozzie. Interesting. Maybe I even know somebody knows something about this Makrow guy. Ain't too many Cetians out in the asteroid belt. Ain't supposed to be any at all, right? One thing I'm not clear on: you want me to help you find a needle in a haystack, then grab it without getting stabbed?" He was using my own metaphor. I guess humans have a limited number of analogies in Standard Anglo-Hispano. I nodded, glad to see how well we understood each other. "But all you offer me is to spring me from this force-field cage so as I can spend the rest of my life with an electronic dog collar."

"Plus we erase your record. You get a clean slate," I added, suspecting he was going to turn me down. But I wasn't about to give up.

"A clean slate." Vasily cleared his throat loudly and spat on the immaculate pseudo-wood floor of the cell. The nano-components built into the phony parquet began bustling around the little puddle of sputum, absorbing it with the efficiency you'd expect from alien tech. He looked on with a hatred bordering on tenderness. "Oh, pardon my manners. I just can't get used to this air conditioning," he said snidely. "Besides, the little bugs are fun to watch."

I summarized our situation: "In other words, you want more." We were off to a good start—and he still hadn't found out that Makrow 34 was a freak just like him, except a thousand times worse. "All right. We might be able to negotiate the collar. A portion of the time, anyway."

"Give it a break, machine-boy. I'm locked up here, sure, but I'm alive. You ain't told me what's so special about this Cetian, but he's gotta be real, real dangerous." If I had a genuine throat, I would have gulped. "Don't tell me there ain't nothing special about him, either. I ain't so dumb as I look. Damned if I'll jump out of the frying pan so as I land in the fire. I don't know the strength of my own Gaussical power—I was just starting to test it when they nabbed me. In fact, I only learned what it was called right here in this cell, and that there were others like me. You know how the aliens don't just control human access to their technology but to information, too. The illegal Web is barely a drop in the ocean compared with what they censor from us. Look here, tinman, I'm gonna ask you one question. Yes or no, that's all. Don't try pulling one over on me." His green eyes stared straight into my fake pupils. "If there's anything kept me alive out there, it was my old friend, intuition. Right now she's whispering into my ear that this Makrow 34 guy must be more than a match for me, Gaussically speaking. 'Cause he's gotta be a fucking Gaussical to make you come here looking for me, am I right?"

I nodded, astonished by the soundness of his reasoning. You could tell Vasily had spent a lot of the past three years educating himself. I doubt he'd have been quite so articulate when he first landed in prison. Or so logical.

Fuck it. I told him everything, with all the gory details.

"I knew it." He half-smiled, shaking his head emphatically. "In that case, sorry, my answer's still no. I'm no match for a freak like that. If I coulda took care of you pozzies like you say he did, I wouldn't even be here."

"But he had help," I objected, trying to win him over. "I'll be with you."

"Oh, right. I forgot about that detail. Best reason for me to refuse. Like the Cetian's not bad enough already, you want me to take on a Colossaur too? I never liked the things—half gorilla, half armored tank. No thanks. Plus the human, on top of it all. I don't want to get within a thousand miles of any human crazy enough to shoot at a pozzie and to survive three seconds fighting hand-to-hand with a Colossaur. Even if it was staged."

I looked down. The nanos were finishing up their task. Hardly any traces remained of the enormous gob of spit. My hopes of finding help were vanishing almost as quickly. I decided to play my last card.

"So they were right about you, Vasily, what they put in your file." I tried to sound as disillusioned and as rude as possible. "You're just a coward."

"Better a poor coward and alive than a rich hero and a corpse," he replied, unperturbed.

Failure. I stood up. Like Marlowe, if I was defeated, I could at least go get myself killed in style. "Live your long, miserable cowardly life, Vasily. Don't worry. With or without your help, I'll catch them in the end, if it takes me a thousand years. I'll get them all. The Colossaur, whatever its name is. That monster, Makrow 34. And that human rat, Giorgio Weekman."

Sometimes I think the gods do exist, and at that moment

I'd even have sworn that they loved me in particular. Just as I was turning to leave, Vasily stopped me. I saw a touch of astonishment as well as bottomless spite in his eyes.

"Hold on a sec. Did you say Giorgio Weekman? Weekman the smuggler?"

"Yeah. We ID'd him on the video," I said, going over both of their files in my mind. No, not a hint that the two knew each other—but recorded facts, as complete as they pretend to be, are never more than a pale reflection of reality. A map isn't the landscape it reflects; a résumé isn't the person it describes.

"Gimme that gizmo." Standing up, he reached for the collar. "When do we leave?"

"Right now." I handed it to him. Sometimes everything falls into place. Could this be the famous "detective's intuition"? Who could say. "So you know this Weekman fellow? Have any idea where he might be?"

"Do I ever." Vasily Fernández grabbed the collar and turned it over in his hands a couple of times. Slim hands, long fingers, more like a concert pianist's than a criminal's. "What'd you say your name was, pozzie?"

"Raymond," I quickly replied, then went on: "Did you and Weekman ever work together?"

"We were supposed to, pozzie," he answered thoughtfully. "But that pig son-of-an-alien left me holding the bag. After he stole everything out of it—all my life savings, gone. You think I'm so stupid or so green I didn't know I'd be falling into a trap by coming to the *Burroughs*? I came because I didn't have a choice, Dick Tracy. Too many of the wrong people knew me, all over the Solar System, for me to start over from scratch somewhere else."

"So we're in this together?" I held out my hand for him, as I'd seen the detectives in Spillane's movie collection do when they were making a deal.

But he didn't take it. Placing the portable anti-Psi generator around his neck, he snapped it shut without hesitation. It made a loud click. I made a mental note of his interesting ability to handle tech gear he'd never seen before. The people who wrote up his file were evidently so frightened by his Gaussical powers that they forgot human beings sometimes have (or learn) more than one skill.

"Yeah, sure. You might say we're in it together, Raymond," Vasily sighed, calling me by my name for the first time. He rolled his head a few times as if to get used to the new bauble around his neck. "Now I know how dogs must feel," he muttered. "But under one condition," he went on, looking me in the eye. "I don't care what you do with the Cetian when we meet up with the merry trio. But Weekman, he's mine. No discussion, or the deal's off."

That worried me. "You aren't thinking of. . . ?" His face told me clearly that he was. "But you've never killed anyone, Vasily," I reminded him, a little astonished to see in living color what I'd read in so many novels: that revenge can push a man to do things no other feelings could.

"I am," he said grimly. "There's a first time for everything, ain't there?" He ran his hand along the collar. "After all, if I'm never really going to be free, thanks to something I never wanted and couldn't help having, what difference does it make if I have to live in the shadows because of something I've been dreaming of doing these past three years?"

I didn't know what to tell him. I suppose, from a human point of view, he was right. So I changed the subject. "Do you have any clues about where to find Weekman?"

He laughed. "Me have clues? You forget I been stuck inside here for three years. But I got a good idea of where to start *looking* for clues. I've also had three years to think it over. We'll go see Old Man Slovoban. What he don't know about underworld business in the Solar System ain't worth finding out."

SIX

SIX THOUSAND MILES before approach orbit our escort changed course so as not to blow our cover. A few minutes later we saw the *Estrella Rom* loom ahead, right where the radar said it should be, blossoming from a blurry, flickering glow into a small ring and finally a large, not quite geometrically correct wheel. It looked so fragile and was spinning so fast on its axis I thought it was a miracle it didn't go to pieces.

"You're flying too fast—and why won't you use the automatic approach system? Don't forget, my special authorization isn't valid on Earth," I reminded Vasily one more time while his hands danced across the controls, working to synchronize our shuttlecraft's angular momentum with the ramshackle docking bay of this unlikely independent orbital station.

The idea of flying in on a broken-down space jalopy confiscated from a ring of spice smugglers—not a nice new police frigate—was Vasily's, of course. He said it was the only way we'd meet the mysterious Old Man. From the little he'd told me, this guy knew everything about dirty business. Giorgio Weekman's business in particular. More than likely he had even heard something about Makrow 34. But he wasn't the sort of guy you could approach in an official capacity, that much was obvious. He didn't like to connect to the Web either. Our best bet was interviewing him in person, old-school style, on his own turf.

Muhammad coming to the mountain. No surprise there. If the mountain tried coming to Muhammad there'd be a landslide.

"Chill. The orbital ain't planet Earth, Raymond," he reminded me in turn, using my name for the second time since we'd met. He hadn't been exactly communicative during our two days flying from the *Burroughs* to this terrestrial orbital. He seemed to think spending all his time on the Web, getting up to speed on current affairs, was more urgent than wasting it talking to me. For my part, I worried that even with a couple of police frigates escorting us, he'd stop helping me if I got in his way. The one time I did try, he called me Dick Tracy again. "Anyways, you know your problem ain't the limits they put on you, it's the xenophobe crazies. I'm docking manual because we look suspicious enough coming here in a practically brand-new ship. You mighta found something older, more beat-up. Ain't too many automatic control shuttlecraft—or pilots in their right mind—who'd get anywheres near this piece-of-shit station. Except pigs. Earthling police. I don't wanna make an old friend feel sorry 'cause he shot me down—especially as it's been so long since we seen each other."

I took a long, uneasy look at the clumsy patchwork of junkyard scrap they called a space station and shrugged. There was no sign of a defense system, which didn't mean there wasn't one. They could keep antimatter minicannons hidden behind any of those sheets of old metal. Or worse. From what I'd heard, these independent stations had exceptionally effective protective mechanisms.

"I guess they don't get too many visitors. At any rate, I'm not too crazy about coming to a station that could fall to bits just from docking with it. I really hope they haven't forgotten you. And let me remind you that everything up to 10,000 miles above the planet's surface is considered its sovereign territory, under the laws of the Solar System. Besides, can you guarantee that somebody crazy enough to live in a heap like that isn't also a rabid xenophobe with an itchy trigger finger?" I felt especially satisfied to be able to slip that old Chandlerian slang into my speech. That's what Marlowe might have said in my shoes.

Vasily didn't answer. He couldn't. Docking a shuttlecraft by hand isn't the sort of thing you can do without giving it your full attention—if you're a human and organic, not a pozzie with a high-powered computer for a brain.

But I have to hand it to El Ex-Afortunado: he managed it pretty well, even though the anti-Psi collar kept him from using his powers. Especially considering he'd just spent three years imprisoned, unable to handle a shuttlecraft control panel except in simulations. We docked on our fourth attempt, just a few scratches on the hull the worse. Instead of the soft click that a similar maneuver with any normal ship would have caused on the *Burroughs*, the racket ringing across the cabin sounded more like a meat grinder trying to sing opera, off-key. Under any other circumstances I would have rated it "extremely worrisome," but one look at Vasily convinced me that, here, this must be the ordinary routine.

The builders and residents of the *Estrella Rom* apparently had the same careless attitude toward systems maintenance as they did toward space engineering and everything else. I remembered the warning that flashed on-screen before the start of at least half the detective videos Spillane loaned me: *The film you are about to see is a reconstruction based on a number of worn copies.* They should inscribe that over this whole station, in capital letters.

If anybody on board knows how to read and write, I mean.

"Well, here we are." Vasily wearily took his hands off the controls and strapped on a cartridge belt so full of ammo it would have embarrassed a professional twentieth-century mafia hit man. I watched him with resentment. He'd insisted on getting back his whole personal artillery stockpile, and when I refused he threatened to trash the deal. I had to give in. But two masers, an infrasonic stun gun, a mini-rocket launcher, a pocket crossbow, and especially his old large-caliber chemical-munition revolver with the laser scope seemed a bit over the top to me. "I hope his damn hypertrophic osteopathy hasn't done in Slovoban, that old fossil. And I hope the Old Man will understand he has to give us a couple pieces of information if he wants to get to know his great-great-great-great-grandchildren. Follow me and don't open your mouth any more than you have to. They don't like guys poking around here asking too many questions." I was about to say something, but he stopped me with a commanding gesture. "Zip it. The rules here ain't the *Burroughs* rules. If you can say there's any rules at all."

He was the criminal (or "former" criminal), the one who knew his way around the place, so I kept my mouth shut and followed. But I had a huge pile of questions I was dying to ask. Hypertrophic osteopathy? The only thing I had about it in my data bank was a brief mention of a rare pituitary disease—and no cases of it had been reported since the aliens revolutionized human medical care. Was the Old Man one of those fundamentalist diehards who refused to accept any technology that had non-human origins? And . . . great-great-great-great-grandchildren? The surprisingly spare information about the *Estrella Rom* stored in my database said Slovoban was the name of the Romani chieftain who had founded the station, in a drunken stupor or a fit of madness, it was unclear which—but that was ninety-six years ago. Could this mean—?

The lack of gravity around the central docking bay didn't surprise me. The *Estrella Rom* had been constructed (so to speak; "agglomerated" or "amassed" would be more accurate) using the oldest and cheapest design capable of simulating something like gravity: a wheel.

Okay, that was the basic design of the *Burroughs*, too, but there the similarity ended. The *Estrella Rom* spun like crazy on its axis to generate enough centrifugal force to keep all the calcium in its inhabitants' bones from leaching out. No cutting-edge alien tech here. No gravity generators, no variable acceleration zones to facilitate coupling with arriving ships. There's no way to know whether the designer intended to add those things later on to his gypsy paradise but ran out of funds, or whether he simply didn't give a damn that the residents of his little world would have to choose between weightlessness and being dizzy all the time.

We passed through an airlock that Yuri Gagarin would have found old-fashioned. The *Estrella Rom* looked even more makeshift on the inside than it did on the outside. Now hanging on by a metal ring that wouldn't have looked out of place in a Bronze Age museum exhibit, now pushing off with one foot from a tin plate on which I could still read the faded letters of an antediluvian earthling soda pop ad, Vasily floated and rebounded with simian agility. If I hadn't known he'd been locked in an anti-Psi cell for the past three years, I would have assumed he'd spent his whole life leaping like a mountain goat. Jump, rebound, push off—until, as we moved farther from the center, his feet began to be attracted, only weakly at first, by one of the bulkheads.

I imitated him, silently startled to find seams joined with rivets, superglue, solder. I had read of such things only in history surveys. In the *Burroughs*, as in all the ships that docked there, they only used universal joints and molecular diffusion seams. When I noticed a pair of ancient plates joined with staples and waterproofed with something that looked exactly like a wad of used chewing gum, I decided to stop getting astonished, to avoid short-circuiting my positronic net.

I couldn't help it, though. The farther Vasily and I went into the labyrinth of passageways and forking paths in the station (it turned out to be much larger on the inside than seemed possible), the looks of the people we passed made the improvised architecture appear almost normal by comparison.

When I first heard this was an independent Romani orbital I may have had the naïve impression that I'd find it full of campfires, mustachioed fiddlers with polka-dotted bandannas around their heads and daggers in their belts, barefoot dancers, knife fights, trained bears—who knows what I was expecting. Anything but this outlandish exhibition of space suits, each more worn-out and patched-up than the last (even the best of them would never have passed muster on the *Burroughs*; some EVA suits didn't even appear to have oxygen tanks), and almost without exception virtually coated in monograms, stickers, and buttons from every imaginable source, from ancient Russian stamps celebrating the prehistoric Interkosmos program to logos for the ephemeral Asteroidal Republic of Ceres, not to mention flags and national emblems for every country past and present, from New Botswana to the Valles Marineris Federation on Mars.

Everybody carried their helmets dangling carelessly from their belts, or at best in place but with the faceplates raised. All the same, they seemed ready and able to respond in a matter of seconds if the aging and over-patched station hull suffered a loss of structural integrity.

Some casually nodded at Vasily in passing. A pair of guys, one shaved bald and one with dreadlocks floating like a halo around his head, even exchanged a couple of words with him. It sounded like Standard Anglo-Hispano but with an exotic syntax and substandard pronunciation, and half the words weren't even in my vocabulary. At least, not with the meanings they seemed to give them.

"Hey, gachó, fresh from the tank?"

"Me likes tu tail, Vas, buratino palsie now?"

"Salve, Jor, what kinda cachorros?"

"Tough monga, Vas, take care tu greenshell. The Old Man te espera."

During a pause I asked him about this curious language and about the second-rate space suits I saw everywhere, almost all of which looked incapable of doing their job.

He shrugged. "Oh, that. I forget you're a greenshell. A novato, I mean. A newbie, a newcomer. That's the old Rom jargon mixed with prison slang. Every subculture creates its own language, and these guys are real good at it. But luckily I speak a little of their dialect, and there's always a sub-lingua franca that all the sabandijas in the system speak, like Anglo-Hispano for misfits. They're on top of what's happening. News spreads faster than light here—not only because of the illegal Web. They already knew I got sprung, and they can see you ain't just a greenshell, you're a pozzie— what they call a buratino. And the space suits? Of course they work, believe it or not. Good thing, too. Everything you see here has been holding up to micrometeorites for nearly a century, and they've never given it a good maintenance check or overhauled it como Dios manda. Plates are always failing, joints lose their seal, solder splits," Vasily muttered with another shrug. "Oh, space isn't what it used to be. But if Magellan could cross the old oceans of Earth in a leaky boat, why should these guys worry? If the hull springs a leak they hold their breath, plug it, and celebrate with home brew. Till it's time to plug the next leak. At least they're free here; they don't pay taxes or serve in any army but their own."

I didn't think freedom could make up for some sorts of deprivation, but I didn't say so. We continued making our way through chambers and corridors until the minutes seemed to turn into hours. The farther we got from the axis, the stronger the centrifugal pseudogravity. The vagrants in space suits began to alternate with small family groups, settled more or less permanently in scattered cubicles on either side of the route we were taking. Now I did begin to see campfires, polka-dot bandannas, and here and there even a pet that seemed to feel as much at home as its masters, both adults and children. I was thankful now that the aliens hadn't given me a sense of smell. If they smelled anything like as bad as they looked, it was a miracle Vasily's stomach hadn't turned inside out like a sock.

Rank-smelling or not, they were all busy with their own affairs (so it seemed) and didn't give us more than the occasional sidelong glance.

At last we reached a door that had a pair of guards posted in front. With its burnished sheen and solid, mass-produced appearance, the door stood out in that run-down setting.

I recognized the model. I'd have to have been blind not to, given my photographic memory. It was a B-378 reinforced diaphragm hatch from the armored passageway of a Tribuno-class interplanetary destroyer. Knowing this did nothing to help me understand what it was doing here. Even in the chaos of Earth, as we'd always heard it described in comparison to the *Burroughs*, you assumed a civilian wouldn't have access to military-grade equipment. Especially not anything this sophisticated.

In the same way, it made no sense to have two sentinels outfitted in Grendel-class combat armor, the flawless finish of their polished mimetic polycarbon contrasting implausibly with the pitiful caricatures of space suits worn by the other station occupants. But in an odd way, standing in front of that door made the two armored giants look more congruous.

The door did not open and the armor-bearing behemoths did not move one nanometer when we showed up. But their array of servo-assisted weapons turned and pointed straight at us. I didn't find this reassuring.

"Entrance to the Old Man's quarters," Vasily whispered nervously. "They've always let me through. But now they see me with you—anybody can smell the alien-flunky on you from ten miles away. I really don't know—"

"Before you say it: don't even think of trying to give me the slip," I warned him. "I don't care if my shell is green or ripe or rotten. I'm your shadow. If they don't let you in—well, I always thought it was a crazy idea to come all the way from Titan to an Earth orbital to check out a possible lead from some space Methuselah about a hidey-hole in the asteroid belt."

"Buratino, sometimes the longest way is the only practical one," Vasily whispered, glancing from the corner of his eye at the guards' impassive armored hulks. "Man, they're taking their time checking us out. If all this is just to tell me I'm not welcome around here, they might as well speed it up."

All of a sudden the two doorkeepers stepped aside with a choreographic precision that displayed their excellent training (one more incongruence: Storm Troopers on the *Estrella Rom*?). The diaphragm-door yawned wide, its blades overlapping one another as they spun to the outer perimeter of the circle, revealing a long tunnel with a fixed rail along the ceiling from which dangled a number of hold bars. Without hesitation, Vasily passed through and grabbed onto one of the bars with both hands. Again I copied him. The door circled shut behind us. I was not at all prepared for what happened next.

Without any warning, the hold bars began to run along the rail, sweeping us through the tunnel faster and faster. Instead of running straight, the route described a broad spiral. Somebody had modified the hell out of what had originally been a short reinforced passageway on a destroyer, making it at least a hundred times longer. Holding onto the bar was no problem for me, but judging by the tension in Vasily's neck and shoulder muscles this jungleland express couldn't have been easy even for someone who was used to it. After a couple of seconds we hit an acceleration of nearly 4 g, and only then did we begin braking, coming at last to a complete stop. The weightlessness told me we'd returned to the center of the great wheel, taking less than five seconds to undo all the work we'd done to get to the door. Start at the center, take a million detours, end up in the same place.

The Old Man was very concerned about security, that much was obvious. But I was surprised to discover that he also knew something about history. The ancient Mycenaean labyrinth-fortresses were built on the same principle, largely forgotten in the later history of fortifications on Earth, but neatly adapted here to space.

We emerged from the tunnel and swam in the air through another diaphragm hatch, this one unguarded. When it closed behind us we found ourselves floating in an enormous, bare, hemispherical chamber. The curved wall seemed to be made of composite ceramic armor, but I couldn't see any furnishings or anything special in it except for a circular mirror, almost thirty feet across, which covered the entire flat side opposite the entrance.

"Slovoban didn't get to be his age by being careless," Vasily snorted, wiping the sweat from his brow. "Hell, I've made this trip at least a hundred times, but he keeps making me go through all this shit. If I didn't think the Old Man was the only one who could help us find the damn Cetian, I would have saved myself the trouble. When he understands that keeping this space dump in one piece depends on how cooperative he is, I hope he'll tell us everything. If not, the frigates we left back there can use the *Estrella Rom* for target practice."

"What makes you think that this senile gypsy, even if his home depends on it, can tell us where—" I was beginning to splutter, spinning in midair to face Vasily, when a third voice stopped me cold.

"We've been friends a long time, Vasily. You don't have to threaten me with the ridiculous pair of frigates you left behind if you want to ask for a favor. Asteroid G 7834 XC. It doesn't even have a name. The orbital data are in the old registers of the Asteroidal Republic of Ceres Mining Company—though they never got around to settling there. And rightly so: there's no mineral wealth on that asteroid; it's just a ball of dust and ice, too dirty for even the water to be usable. But that's where Weekman kept his smuggling base, ten years ago. If you hurry you might still find him holed up there with Makrow 34 and their overgrown reptilian friend, counting their loot."

The voice was soft but booming, with an indescribable, almost liquid quality to it. I spun about so abruptly that, forgetting the weightlessness, I crashed into the wall.

The mirror had turned transparent. Two-way: an old but always effective trick. Looking through it, I saw another hemispherical room, the twin of the one we were in. But that room was crowded with things.

Its decor was . . . striking. The walls were entirely covered with two basic motifs.

The first: complex, advanced, modern-looking electronic devices that ten minutes earlier I would have thought entirely out of place in a junkheap orbital like the *Estrella Rom*. I can't call myself anything like an expert on the subject, but to me they appeared to be highly sophisticated life-support systems. I should have been surprised to see them there, but after the two Grendel-class Storm Trooper outfits, the armored diaphragm hatch, and the spiral tunnel, I felt ready not to be shocked if I found out that one of those contrivances was capable of generating a hyperspace portal.

In any case, I found the second decor element even more intriguing.

Suits of armor.

Not just titanic composite Grendels and other modern, sophisticated, super-costly servo-assisted combat systems, but also genuine historical relics. I'm not an expert on armor either, but photo-recall does have its uses. I recognized an armored samurai suit, probably fifteenth-century, and medieval European armor that I thought might be of Burgundian make. The others I could only speculate about with the boldness of a dilettante: one might have been Mongol, or perhaps Burmese; another Roman legionnaire or maybe Scythian; the next was either Celtic or Viking. A fine collection.

They all looked authentic, except for one detail suggesting that, though one or another of them may actually have been genuine antiques, most had to be mere reproductions (and splendid ones) made on order for the eccentric collector (I wondered that Vasily hadn't mentioned this curious side of the Old Man to me).

The detail was their size. The medieval armor looked a bit large, and as far as I know Roman legionnaires weren't known for their height, nor were most medieval Mongols six and a half feet tall. But even a Colossaur would have found the servo-assisted Grendel suit cumbersome. Nobody under eleven feet could have used it comfortably.

"Your friend Slovoban's a funny sort of guy," I said to Vasily, turning to him with my most ironic expression. "Setting aside his paranoia, did he have some of these suits of armor made for his collection in size XXL to impress his visitors? Doesn't strike me as necessary, given the pair of gargantuan doorkeepers we passed back there."

Vasily's sudden silence, but above all the look of reverence that came over his face, told me that the Old Man must have entered his own reception room. I turned back, and indeed, there between the life-support systems and the enormous historical suits of armor, a man had just made his appearance.

Or something that had once, long ago, been a man. Because Adam wouldn't have readily recognized this stick-thin cross between a spider and a snake as one of his descendants.

Okay, no need to exaggerate. He wasn't all that ugly. I've seen mutant eel larvae that looked uglier and moved with less grace.

Not many, though.

One look at him and I understood that Vasily's term, hypertrophic osteopathy, was right on the money. The largest suits of armor weren't oversized, as I'd thought.

Unbelievable as it was, they were the small ones that had sadly become too short.

In his heyday, Old Man Slovoban must have already been a fairly tall man, maybe six, even six and a half feet tall, judging from the oldest suits in his collection. Living in weightlessness for so many decades, the expansion of his intervertebral discs and articular stretching due to the weakening of his skeletal structure through calcium loss might have added another four inches. But this *thing* stood more than eleven and a half feet tall from head to toe.

He had not merely grown taller.

Many years of weightlessness could have made his muscles atrophy a little—but not to this extent. He was hardly more than skin and bones. His ribs, having lengthened and softened through some teratological process, seemed to have folded and interwoven themselves around his shrunken torso, within which his heart and lungs, freed from the struggle against gravity, also seemed to have shrunk. The intravenous feeding tube emerging from his neck gave me a clear idea of what had happened to his stomach.

Beyond this, he was pale to the point of translucence, and his arms, long and noodle-thin, were quietly folded into impossible angles, as if they had more joints than any normal human limbs—or were a veritable showcase of fractures. Perhaps osteoporosis and osteochondritis as well?

Even his facial features had changed drastically. The cartilage growth typically seen in old age had reached such an extreme, whether because of the lack of gravity or the horrible hypertrophy, that the enormous bat ears and the nose curved like a crow's beak made him look more like a wicked goblin than a Homo sapiens. And his entire cranium, if that was still the right word for the enormous, vaguely globular form, barely confined by impossibly flexible bones, reminded me more of the soft, shapeless head of an octopus than a hominid.

The worst, most monstrous part of it was that behind all these extreme transformations you could still recognize the original human form, little of which remained now beyond this grotesque spectral parody.

I stared as if hypnotized. And used all my self-control to refrain from shooting him. Hypertrophic osteopathy or not, the mere existence of this being was a terrible crime according to the aliens' laws (which I was sworn to uphold). If I were to fulfill my duty to the letter, I'd have to administer euthanasia to him without delay. Such extreme variations on the human biotype were categorically banned, not only on the *Burroughs* but throughout the Solar System.

But I was certain this deformation must have been caused by disease. It couldn't possibly be a case of genetic modification. No human could have wanted to have turned into . . . that.

And when the aliens kept a close eye on a thing, like they did with genome stability, you didn't want to mess around with it. The terrestrial police might allow an "independent" enclave like the *Estrella Rom* or the *Angel of Zion* to orbit their planet and traffic in contraband replacement parts, pirated software, drugs, things like that, if they felt like it. But they'd never risk reprisals against their entire species such as the aliens threatened if they discovered some crazy person playing at genetic manipulation with human DNA.

All Vasily said was, "Thanks, Old Man." He touched me softly on the shoulder and whispered, "It's done. And stop staring at him, he'll get annoyed. We know where to look for them now. We can go."

"Don't worry about it, Afortunado, I'm used to being seen for what I am: a freak." The old man's voice spoke out once more in the spluttering, underwater tone that characterized his toothless mouth. "No need to be in such a rush. Ah, Vasily. How long's it been since we met—five years, no? Aren't you even going to ask me why I gave you the info you came for before you had time to ask? Or what it is I want?"

"In the orphanage I learned not to abuse my good luck, Old Man," Vasily said, smiling. "But I admit to a certain curiosity."

"*I admit to a certain curiosity.* How your vocabulary has grown in that cell, Vasily," the Old Man joked as he snaked past his collection, caressing some of the suits with his impossibly flexible arms. "And your buratino friend is very curious as well. He's thinking: it must be illegal for a human monstrosity like me, unable to withstand Earth's gravity for even a second, to exist."

"Oh, not at all," I began, feeling even more uncomfortable, if possible. Could this monster be a telepath, too?

But the Old Man stopped me with a majestic wave of his hand.

"I knew I'd live to see this day." He smiled, if the catfish yawn of his toothless mouth could be called a smile. "I knew he'd break every limit one of these days. You can fool the human police, but not the aliens, or their robot bootlickers. Afortunado, I gave the information because I wanted to make you the instrument of my revenge."

"Oh," Vasily said simply, looking uneasy. "Well. My pleasure."

"I am Slovoban. The Old Man. I founded the *Estrella Rom*. I dreamed of a space in space for those who had no space. Such as my people. That was ninety-six years ago. My brain is the only part of me that I've kept in perfect condition, but it makes up for everything I've had to renounce. Because for forty-four years I was the invincible patriarch of all space tramps. No man could beat me in a one-on-one fight. No cheat could catch me up with any of his tricks. Perhaps no one recalls it today, but fifty-two years ago I was not this pitiful shapeless thing."

The eyes of the living mummy closed, dreaming, covered by almost transparent lids, and his arachnid fingers ran along the feathers on his Aztec (or maybe Inca, I'm not sure) breastplate.

"No; when I had this place built, I was Slovoban El Rayo. Six foot four, weighed two hundred ninety pounds. Reflexes of a wildcat. I had forgotten more things about hand combat than you'll ever learn, Vasily. I was the best. With a knife, a cudgel, exotic weapons, or my bare hands. In duels I killed twenty-three men who challenged my authority, until there were none left who dared take me on. I was the chief, the present day was my fiefdom, and the future my kingdom. The aliens had just arrived in the Solar System with their faster-than-light ships and all the rest of their omnipotent technology. I saw the troubled waters and thought I'd try my hand at fishing, too, forgetting that sometimes troubled waters are full of sharks. I went in on a deal involving smuggled universal energy crystals with some Cetians. . . ."

I listened transfixed, knowing where the Old Man wanted to take us. Just like one of Marlowe's investigations: it always turns out everybody has business to settle with the bad guy. Fifty-six years is a long time in human terms, but barely a blink of an eye in a Cetian's life cycle; they only look like humanoids. They hatch from eggs in litters of up to fifty clones and can live for five millennia.

Fifty-six years. Of course. I hadn't heard anything about that little gap between the date of Makrow 34's criminal activity and his capture and escape, thanks as always to the aliens' love for compartmentalizing information. In this case I was up against three enemies and loads of traitors. And I still didn't really know which side to count Vasily El Afortunado on.

". . . but I miscalculated." Old Man Slovoban tried to shrug, but with his softened skeleton the gesture was reduced to a semiliquid amoeba-like tremble. "I had met somebody tougher than me. Behind the Cetian's delicate body and doll face, there was a real demon."

Here came laughter that sounded more like a hoarse cough.

"He pulled one over on me; he challenged me to a knife fight in zero gravity. I accepted. Nobody handled a knife better than I did. But I don't think any human ever made so many clumsy mistakes in a fight that his life depended on. I don't know how it could have happened. Every time I was about to get him, something went wrong. I ended up with two wounds—I, who had never been touched by an enemy's blade. One I gave myself, in my arm, when it cramped up inexplicably. The other was a disaster. My knife hit the metal wall, sparks flew, they blinded me temporarily—and just then he threw his dagger and hit my thigh, right in the femoral artery."

The Old Man's dim eyes flashed.

"At least I was lucky enough not to lose the leg. Incredible aim, skill, or luck. You know how hard it is to throw a knife in zero gravity and hit what you aim for?" He sighed. "I've never understood how I had so much bad luck that day. And there's not much else to tell. Makrow 34 ran off with all the contraband while I was unconscious. Also, his stiletto was laced with poison. My doctors couldn't even figure out what kind of venom he used. I had to spend a mountain of money and hire a Grodo biochemist, who finally identified it, though he was unable to counter it completely. All he could tell me was that it was a toxin from an exotic Rigelian anemone. A strange recombinant substance with no known antidote. Completely illegal throughout the galaxy. Not lethal, but insidious. Its curious effects have turned me into this thing that I am now."

He waved his long, boneless limbs.

"Hypertrophic osteopathy and muscular degeneration, its primary effects, aren't fatal if you take good care of yourself, though they are extremely inconvenient. But every sword has two edges: the effects of the genetic venom have also extended my life long enough for me to see the day when the aliens themselves avenge me."

My pity for this man who had never forgotten his first, last, and only defeat prompted me to reveal the one piece of information I should have kept the most secret. "It wasn't bad luck, Old Man. Makrow 34 had Psi powers." And I explained what a Gaussical is while Vasily wrung his hands nervously and kept glancing sidelong at me.

"Ah." The Romani centenarian's eyes shined brighter than ever and his toothless mouth twisted into another parody of a grin. "A Psi. A damnable probability manipulator. Interesting, I didn't know such things existed. That explains my clumsiness, his luck, his good aim, everything." He cough-laughed again and ran his hand distractedly over another of his suits of armor. "That explains—everything," he repeated.

For a few long seconds an uncomfortable silence hung over us all. At last Vasily broke it, nervous. "Well. It's been a long time since we met, and I'm really sorry, Old Man," he said simply. "But we're in a rush. You wouldn't want that monster to get away, would you? Rest easy. I won't tell anybody about this, you know? And I'll bring you his heart—if the Cetian has one."

"Cetians have two, in their abdomens," I explained, and felt ridiculous for having done so.

"Better—one for you, one for me," Slovoban joked. "Good luck to you, kid, and to your positronic friend, too. And be careful with that Makrow. I knew he was dangerous, but if he's a Psi, you'll have to keep all your eyes on him—and more than four eyes would be better. I'd say, more like ten. May God and a loaded maser always be with you." With that, the hatch reopened and the interview was over.

We retraced our entire route through the tunnel and the filthy labyrinths of the Romani space station back to our shuttle in silence. It was only when we had left the *Estrella Rom* behind us that El Ex-Afortunado spoke again. "Thanks, Raymond."

"For what?" His thanks had taken me by surprise. My train of thought had already moved on to the idea of asking for reinforcements to take Asteroid G 7834 XC. Two police frigates should do it, but only if they were carrying at least a couple of anti-Psi field generators. I hadn't done any. . . .

"For what you did," Vasily said. "For giving Slovoban back some of his pride. And especially for not telling him I'm a Gaussical too." He gulped. "I never dared to tell him. I know it'll sound weird, but if I've ever had anything like a father, it was him, and I'd hate it if he associated me in any way with the guy who reduced him to that."

I looked at him with curiosity, but I guessed that this was not the right time to ask for explanations. The mysteries of human nature. Sometimes I think the more I know them, the less I understand them.

SEVEN

AFTER STUFF HAPPENS, any idiot with enough time to waste can analyze what went right, what turned out badly, the reasons behind each mistake, and which brilliant move could have made the difference at each point, turning failure into triumph. Any elementary school student could tell Napoleon when to move his artillery, when to call for Murat's cavalry, and how to maneuver his troops so he could thumb his nose at Wellington in Waterloo. Any halfway competent amateur could advise Lee on how to defeat Grant in Gettysburg or tell Hannibal how to bring Rome to its knees with his elephants.

But in the whirlwind of events, generals not only don't know where their enemies have their strongest troop concentrations, often they aren't even very clear about where their own forces are. So a battle in real time is nothing like a chessboard with all the pieces moving in the open. It's more like a knife fight between two blindfolded opponents, each trying to stab the other, guided only by the sound of their breathing while trying to hold their own breath so the other guy won't stab them.

All this is just a fancy but futile attempt to excuse myself for the total disaster that was our attempt to overrun asteroid G 7834 XC.

It couldn't even remotely be called a battle. An ambush, a massacre, maybe even a firing squad. Could it have been avoided? Of course—if I had been a clairvoyant, I might have known that Makrow 34, Weekman, and the Colossaur had planned for exactly such a massive operation. Or if I'd been a brilliant strategist and tactician like Hannibal, Napoleon, Grant, or even his defeated foe Lee, I might have calmly called off the reinforcements and anti-Psi fields and instead attempted a much more low-key incursion. A standard commando action: just Vasily, me, and at most a couple human police as backup. Maybe we would have at least stood a chance.

But when the aliens designed us they forgot to include clairvoyance among our powers. And even the nearly omniscient Slovoban had no way of knowing that the diabolical Cetian and his accomplice Giorgio had invested half their fraud and smuggling profits not in energy crystals but in turning that remote asteroid, their "temporary base," into a lethal trap.

The other thing is that, even though we were the invaders, they held the advantage of surprise. Neither the human police nor I myself really expected to find the fugitives on the forsaken chunk of rock that the Old Man had indicated. Maybe it was because I had read too many Conan Doyle-style detective stories, but it seemed most likely that I'd show up at an empty lair and have to deal with a complicated jigsaw puzzle of false trails, red herrings, and incomplete clues that would seem impossible to reconstruct at first, until with a brilliant flash of insight I discovered the meaning of some words in an exotic language or of some intriguing signs or drawings, leading me at last to the criminals after a long string of adventures.

That would have been good, maybe, but too Conan Doyle, too S. S. Van Dine. I should also have been paying attention to Chandler and Hammett. As I might easily have learned from Philip Marlowe's literary adventures, in real life you don't solve crimes by deciphering clues written in dead languages but, almost always, by a moment of carelessness on the bad guy's part, a chance meeting on the street, a betrayal, a coincidence—in other words, luck.

First, the idea that we could find the bad guys' hidden lair so easily, just by following a tip from the Methuselah of the Romani; then, the idea that they'd be dumb enough to stay there, as if they couldn't guess the Old Man would know how Weekman was linked to Makrow 34, as if they didn't know he ached for revenge and would tell us where they were, and I'd get help from criminals in the pen—it all seemed too foolish, too simplistic, too easy. Almost like a trick.

But life is a great trickster, because there they were. Even if they weren't exactly waiting for us, even if it came as a bit of a surprise to them when their radar showed a fleet of police ships approaching, they didn't lose their heads. After all, they had long since taken precautions against such an eventuality—and, as we were soon to discover, their preparations were more than adequate, almost excessive.

"I don't like this," Vasily whispered when the motley planetoid resolved into a bleak labyrinth of rock and ice on our screens but we could see no movement on it. "It's too quiet. Gives me the willies."

"Me too," I replied, also in a whisper, under the influence of his conspiratorial tone. "But not to worry, we'll be on our way soon. You can tell they're not here now, if they ever were. It always seemed too easy to have your Old Man send us straight to their evil lair."

A light on my control panel switched from blue to green. I smiled; to think that Vasily had thought this shuttle too new to dock with the *Estrella Rom*, when it didn't even have a centralized warning system, just this primitive set of Christmas-tree lights. A green light could only mean that one of our escorts was requesting a com channel, despite my orders for strict radio silence.

Well, fuck it, they must have also realized we'd made the trip for nothing; there couldn't be anybody here. I opened a reception line. "Calling Raymond, Police Frigate 46 here." The voice of one of the human cops came over the com. "Look at this, pozzie. Doesn't it look like the wreck of one of those ships the bounty hunters use?"

"Wait, what?" I was surprised, more than a little. "Bounce the image to my holoscreen," I was beginning to say . . .

. . . when all hell broke loose.

The asteroid literally exploded. Giant chunks of carbonaceous chondrites and dirty carbon dioxide ice flew in every direction. The clouds of sublimated water vapor were so thick, the explosion even made a sound for an instant. Its muted rumble reached us through the shuttle bulkheads.

At first I thought, "Shit, it's a trap—a hydrogen bomb or something," but I quickly realized that if it had been nuclear I never would have thought anything of it at all. The two blue lights were still blinking on my control panel, meaning that the two frigates hadn't disappeared in the explosion either.

If we were all still safe and sound, the next logical step was for me to ask myself whether it might not be a natural process. Sometimes these compound or conglomerate planetoids simply become unstable when they approach the sun, and the pressure of the sublimated ice inside them produces this sort of explosive effect.

That's when I noticed the bluish sheen of monomolecular ceramics among the asteroidal detritus, then saw it form the unmistakable silhouette of a shark, and I understood three things—all too late.

First, there was nothing natural about this.

Second, I'm a reckless idiot.

And third, the reason why the aliens were so obsessed with catching the Cetian Psi. This was no small-time thug: I don't know if I'll ever find out all the dirty deals Makrow 34 had a hand in, but I was now sure that some of them must have been extremely profitable, because he had made enough to buy parts, smuggle them into the Solar System (the number of customs agents he must have bribed to do so is incredible), and then secretly assemble inside the asteroid the marvel of Colossaur military technology that humans have named a Chimera-class micro-destroyer.

I won't go on and on here about the combat abilities of a Chimera. The point is, it was far too tough a nut to crack for two interplanetary patrol craft and an old human-manufactured shuttle.

One second later, the powerful miniwarship fired the first shot from its particle cannon and put one of the frigates that were supposedly supporting Vasily and me out of commission. The hull of the police craft cracked open like a coconut I once saw on a holovideo that a native expertly sliced in half with a single machete blow.

There the similarities ended: no coconut water or pulp emerged from the two halves, only clouds of air that instantly froze, along with weapons, detritus, . . . and men. I don't think there were any survivors. Even if they had been wearing their pressure suits, unless the suits were armored the explosive decompression would have reduced them to rags.

The remaining police frigate, with a grand display of dutifulness (or of suicidal tendencies), opened fire with all its weapons. Either the crew didn't know what a Chimera could do, or they simply didn't want to pass on to the next world without at least putting a scratch on the pirate ship's casing. In any case, they failed miserably: their microwave beams, missiles, and regulation police lasers bounced harmlessly off the Colossaur destroyer's alternating-field armor.

By contrast, when Makrow and his sidekicks also used all their weaponry in response, they literally annihilated the human ship. I think the biggest fragment that remained would easily have fit inside my hat.

Meanwhile, I was intent on doing the only proper thing under the circumstances: getting out of there, full blast. If the battle is already lost, all you can do is retreat. He who loses and runs away in time can return to fight and win. A coward who escapes lives to become brave. Old sayings with which I was suddenly in complete agreement.

That meant pushing our accelerators to the max with a swipe of my hand, turning off the artificial gravity with a kick of one foot, holding the seat restraints with my teeth, hearing the roar of the plasma engines forced from idle to peak in the blink of an eye—and seeing something that looked a lot like a column of flying ants (ants? in a space shuttle? and flying? where'd they come from?) do a cheerleader routine around the air conditioner vent.

In short: madness, terror, chaos, and putting as many light-years as possible between the Chimera's sharklike profile and us.

And it's not like giving them the slip would be easy. Chimeras are the pride of the Colossaurs' military engineering. Not only are they hyper-armored and bristling with all sorts of weapons, they also have batteries of very effective sensors. Only the swiftness of my positronic neural responses allowed us to escape their first attack, evading microwave beams and hailstorms of charged particles that blasted nearby asteroids into millions of shards of rock and ice.

It wasn't a simulation or a warning shot: the barrage was intended to destroy us. After that first attempt, I knew they were going to pursue us. I swatted away some flying ants and tried to radio for help; by then it didn't matter if the whole Solar System knew where we were. No answer.

The damn Colossaurs clearly didn't forget to include a massive radio interference generator in the arsenal of their Chimeras. Not even God could hear us. Nobody would help us unless we helped ourselves. Makrow didn't want witnesses. After wiping two police frigates off the map, he wasn't about to let us waltz off to the *Burroughs* with news about his latest crime and his newest ship.

A crazy pursuit began through drifting rocks. An obstacle race between the defenseless rabbit and the ferocious wolf, an escape punctuated with volleys that would have blown us to bits if any had hit us—but as if some benevolent god had placed us under his capricious protection, the worst they did was graze us, and only a couple of times at that.

Meanwhile, the impossible ants never stopped buzzing around. Weird. Some of them didn't seem quite normal to me; they had four, even six wings. Mutants?

Aside from that, everything was going bizarrely well. I remember thinking that Makrow 34's powers of probabilistic manipulation might not be effective beyond a certain distance after all. But all the same, I had to perform my full repertoire of prohibited maneuvers (and even create a couple of new ones on the fly). I mentally blessed Vasily and his insistence on remaining loyal to our old shuttle. It might not have had anything remotely as good as the shields on the pirate ship or a regulation frigate. Or their weapons, or half the power of their engines.

But even their small Chimera didn't have much advantage over us in maneuverability, at the low velocities required by an asteroid belt transit. Plus, fortunately, no human, Colossaur, or Cetian pilot is my rival when it comes to reaction speed.

And I'd never reacted so quickly.

Even so, it took us nearly thirty desperate loops, sudden changes in direction, and zigzags around asteroids to lose sight of them, also losing several square feet of our ship's outer shielding in our insane final maneuver: squeezing between a par of planetoids, each of them more than a hundred million tons of rock.

That was the worst moment. Really ugly. Like slipping between Scylla and Charybdis. A rock and a hard place. The maneuver had to be precise to the nanosecond. If we'd bumped into them a fraction of a second sooner, they would have caught our flying junkster between them and ground our hull like the molars of some immense monster—but then I wouldn't be telling this story now. And if I had hesitated a millisecond longer to attempt the passage, the pirate ship's artillery would have reduced us to ashes.

But things worked out like it was the best of all possible worlds. We left the wolf, with its fangs that snarled and its claws that snatched, behind us. Our tortured engines returned to cruising speed. I slowly peeled my hands from the controls. I looked at them: steady as ever. And I thanked the designers of our android bodies for neglecting to give us involuntary muscle spasms, endocrine glands, and sweat. If I had been human, I would have been buzzing with adrenaline, trembling like a leaf, and drenched through like a diving champion's towel. Like Vasily.

"Well, that was a close call," I said, patting his shoulder to calm him and enjoying the elemental pleasure of hearing my own voice. "Who could have imagined they'd have a Chimera hidden in there? Good thing their aim was off and luck was on our side. Makrow must not have been having one of his best days—" Then I saw something in El Afortunado's palm that made me stop short.

The anti-Psi collar. The collar no living being could possibly remove once it had been snapped around his neck.

Okay, so Vasily had done it anyway. A good thing, too.

Now I understood what those flying ants were doing there (indeed, by now they were all gone), and most of all, what was behind our miraculous escape. Psi powers at play once more. Gaussical versus Gaussical. My friend hadn't done anything wrong. How could I have thought otherwise? Analyzed objectively: without his ability to manipulate probabilities, a Chimera taking on a shuttle is a fight between a shark and a sardine. A canned sardine. All the odds were against our survival.

"How...?" I was about to ask him, pointing toward the collar, but he interrupted me.

"Old pickpocket's trick. For all the good it did us. We're still screwed. That Makrow is a lot more powerful than me; I know that now for sure." He pointed at an insistently blinking light on the control panel. "Or he's had more time to practice, especially over the past few days. We got away, but not undamaged." He unfastened the belts on his safety harness and floated across the cabin to the pressure suit closet. Of course: the first system to fail is always the artificial gravity. He gave a long sigh. "If there's one thing I learned when I got caught, it's that sometimes you win, sometimes you lose, but most of the time you win and lose, both at once. Like now. I hope for our sake that whoever owned these suits kept the breathing devices in better shape than my Romani friends—because I think we're going to spend a long, long time stuffed into them."

"Alright, but if they were going to hit us, did it have to be right in our main power generator? Let's see, we have to cut the power cycles or we'll explode." Talking to myself, another custom that I've noticed helps calm the humans at tense moments. I started punching the switches again, turning off the reactor and jettisoning the energy crystals in an attempt to get the damn red radioactive leak indicator light to turn off. At last I managed it—but the cabin lights abruptly went dim, and I cursed again.

Of course the primary electrical system would also have to be disconnected now, too. Luckily, my eyes work in much dimmer light than a human's. The emergency circuit lights gave off a faint yellowish glow under which Vasily's face took on a sickly hue.

"Oof, that was close. How come it hasn't exploded already?" I breathed easier once the alarming red light disappeared from the control panel and a bit of power returned. Not all of it, though. It didn't take a genius to figure out that trying to restart the main engine would leave us completely in the dark. "Well, good thing you noticed in time. We're stuck here, but the life-support system will hold up. All we have to do now is send out a Mayday and they'll find us—sooner or later. That is, if those guys ever turn off their interference curtain."

"They won't. But that isn't why I don't think you should try the radio again." Vasily was already putting on his space suit, an older model but supersophisticated compared with what the Old Man's people were using on the *Estrella Rom*. "It doesn't matter if the support system holds up. We gotta get out of here. With all the energy you jettisoned just now, the Chimera's detectors will find us in no time if they're looking for us, and I guarantee you they are. So after letting them triangulate us with their radio direction finder, you might not even have time to get your suit on—especially if you keep moving so slow." With a snort, he grabbed another suit from the storage space and with a push floated it my way through the darkened cabin. "Come on, Raymond, we don't have time to waste. We'd better be well clear of this shuttle when that warship gets here or shrapnel from the explosion could get us. I know it would take the worst kind of bad luck, but when Gaussicals are involved you never know."

I stared at him. Had he really forgotten that I'm not human? "Thanks for your concern, but I don't need a suit, Vasily." I took off my own safety harness. "Did you forget that pozzies don't breathe?"

"Forget? No way, Dick Tracy," he taunted me as he finished adjusting his suit and locking his helmet on. "How could I? Woulda been real nice for me not to need to breathe either right now. Thing is, we don't know how many days we'll have to float around in this dull asteroid soup before we get picked up, and I'm not planning to go crazy talking to myself the whole time. Big defect in the hyperrealistic android design: you don't have a radio system built into your structure, do you?"

I nodded, understanding at last what he was getting at: maybe I don't need air to exist ("live" wouldn't be quite the right word), but without a hermetically sealed space suit my compressor couldn't supply me with air to talk with, and we wouldn't be able to exchange ideas and keep a grasp on sanity.

In silence I took off my fedora, carefully folded it, placed it in an inner pocket of my trench coat, and started climbing into the old pressure suit. I wondered how Vasily planned to hold a conversation without breaking radio silence. I decided it wouldn't be long before I found out.

EIGHT

"HEY RAYMOND, you asleep?"

"What a question, Vasily—you know I'm not."

"You should try it sometime. Zoning out might do you some good. Tell me something, pozzie: they say the aliens copied you guys' personalities from real humans that got executed. Remember anything about what you were before? Cop or robber? You know I'm joking, but don't you miss having dreams?"

"Cute idea. You think that makes us some sort of resuscitated zombies? No, sorry, those are just rumors floating around the System, Vasily. I was never alive, so I don't miss what I never had. But if you really want to know, sometimes I dream while I'm awake."

"About electric sheep?"

"Good one. I didn't know you were a *Blade Runner* fan. But it so happens I have a friend on the *Burroughs* whose name is Deckard, would you believe it, and he loaned me the novel and the movie. They're both good."

"Wow, a well-educated cop and everything, I'm in luck. Anyways, what do positronic police robots dream about? Catching criminals, or pozzie women?"

"You know we don't have sex, Vasily. But work isn't everything for us, either. For example, right now I'm dreaming how sweet it would be if a micrometeorite cracked your helmet and shut you up, once and for all."

"Ha. Nice. Piece of advice, robot: instead of dreaming, try praying. And you know what? I love you too, Raymond."

We were floating through the infinite void, nothing above and nothing below, our helmets held tight against each other. With his extraordinary engineering skills, Vasily had figured out how to tie us together, harness to harness, so our helmets would be in contact and we could talk. There's no sound in a vacuum, but it travels fine through solids. Vasily's words resonated through my whole suit.

"I always thought there wouldn't be any room to move around in the asteroid belt, but look how empty this is. A guy could die of boredom. I'd even take a comet passing by now and then, it'd make a nice show."

"Vasily, at the speed we're going, we could float for thousands of years even inside the rings of Saturn without running into a particle larger than an atom. Space is mainly a vacuum—didn't they teach you that in school?"

"Yeah, and they also taught me not to squeeze my pimples, and that reality really exists and isn't just an illusion of our senses. But I guess they didn't teach me very well: I've always squeezed my pimples, and don't you think the asteroid belt is maybe as crowded as I said, it's just that we see it like this?"

"You're starting to worry me, Afortunado. Maybe we've been floating here for too many hours. Look me in the eye. That's the way to solipsism. You're starting to deny reality, and you'll end up saying you're God."

" . . . ."

"Don't you go quiet on me, for the love of—whatever it is you love. Talk to me. Dammit, talk to me!"

"Chill, Raymond. I'm not that far gone. Or did you forget I spent three years in the hole on your pretty little station and stayed sane? I was just joking. And I wanted to find out how positronic robots cursed."

"Heh. I love you too, Vasily, you know?"

"Good thing, because as tight as we're tied together, if we didn't love each other—"

The damned destroyer had found our shuttle just five minutes after we abandoned ship. But they didn't open fire and obliterate it, as we had hoped; Makrow was an old dog who knew all the tricks, and he must have known the shuttle would be empty and undefended. In any case, they checked to be sure. We hid behind a couple of frozen clouds and watched as a figure in a pressure suit, which from its enormous size could only have been the Colossaur ex-bagger, left the pirate ship and entered ours. I cursed myself for neglecting to rig up at least an explosive booby trap in the airlock or something. We could have been down one enemy. Like I said, after everything's over it's easy to see where you slipped up.

"Raymond, do you believe in God?"

"Good question. I guess not. It hasn't been proved that such an entity is real. But I don't have enough material to deny his existence either. Let's say: I have no opinion. I'm a skeptic, waiting for evidence."

"I understand. For us humans it's easy: God was the one who created us in his image and likeness. You guys, on the other hand, knowing you're the aliens' creatures—I guess it's better to deny God than to accept a god like that. If I had to pray to a Grodo I'd die of shame."

"It isn't that easy, Vasily. If byzantine arguments and theological muddles are your thing, try this one: God used the aliens and the humans to create us, as a living symbol that we're all equal before Him. I'm not going to defend the idea, but doesn't it seem perfectly possible? We pozzies would be the best of both cultures."

"Hey, buratino, that ain't bad if what you wanna do is pump up your ego. But let's change the subject or I'll start to believe that God created the universe for my own personal suffering. How old are you, Raymond? Did you have any sort of childhood?"

"You gotta stop with the dumb questions. You know perfectly well all pozzies are the same age, fifty-seven. We were all created when the aliens arrived, when the *William S. Burroughs* was built. And we were born—or rather, assembled—as adults. Who would have any respect for a child police officer, even if he was a robot? Better we talk about you, Vasily Fernández. How did you choose this life?"

"Sorry, Raymond, nobody chooses to be a crook. It's what you do for survival when you got no other options. How many possibilities you think a kid like me—no parents, no family—had? Was I supposed to mortgage forty years of my life so a corporation would pay for my studies and let me become an engineer? Or maybe buy a ship, become a trader, and haggle with aliens on your station? Yeah, I could have done that, I guess—but it never occurred to me. I was too worried each morning might be my last. The life of a child alone in the world ain't easy. It don't get any better when you're a teenager alone. So—look here, buddy, let's quit gabbing for a while, before I say a couple of things you wouldn't want to hear."

"Okay, Vasily, as you wish."

After a thorough search to be sure the shuttle was empty, the bad guys blew it up, of course. Good thing we were far away. Then the Chimera started hunting in the vicinity like a shark circling a shipwrecked sailor's raft.

Five days had gone by since then. Not a minute more or less. It occurred to me that having a computer built into your brain can sometimes be a defect. I figured my pal must have already lost his sense of time, if not his mind altogether. In a way I envied him. He was beyond all responsibility. Not me. I had to keep talking to him, constantly, even when he refused to answer: if anything stood between him and madness, it was my being here, always trying to strike up conversations, which began to seem more and more incoherent to me.

"Raymond, where'd we screw up?"

"Huh?"

"You know. Those two novels by your guy Chandler you told me from memory—in the end, the good guys always win. Maybe they get beat up and arrested and worse along the way, but they win. So, what did we do wrong?"

"Well, it isn't all over yet. Sometimes real life isn't like a novel."

"Hey, that was supposed to be my line! Look, I think our problem is, I ain't one of your honest but unorthodox private eyes. I ain't even a cop, just another crook. Fighting fire with fire don't always work, looks like."

"That's not your fault, Vasily. You did your part, and you did it well. You went above and beyond. If you hadn't put your powers to work, most likely we wouldn't be here now, and I'm very grateful to you for it."

"No problem. But for all the fun we're having, they shoulda just gone ahead and fried us with the particle beam. At least it woulda been a quick death."

"Don't be silly. Where there's life, there's hope."

"Raymond, do me a favor, spare me the clichés. At this point, if God himself don't save us, you might be the only one with any hopes of . . . living, if that's what you call it. Tell me: the gas exchange membranes in my tank are filling with toxins, right? How much longer do you think I can hold out?"

"No, Vasily, what are you saying? Everything's fine. You have space paranoia, that's all. Talk to me."

"What if I don't feel like talking?"

"Then I'll talk. Look, let me tell you another Chandler novel you haven't heard yet. It's called *Farewell, My Lovely.*"

"What's it about?"

"A big guy—huge, mammoth, very badly dressed, just got out of prison and he's looking for his little girlfriend."

"Hey, don't sound bad. But no thanks, maybe some other time. Raymond, could I ask you a favor?"

"If it's anything I can do, I'd be happy to, Vasily."

"Shut up for a while. You talk so much I can't hear myself thinking."

The bad guys hadn't called off their search. Makrow and company were patient and meticulous, and they knew what was at stake if they didn't find us. They passed within thirty or forty yards of us a couple of times. Good thing our suits contained hardly any metal and we maintained strict radio silence. Good thing, too, that Vasily's powers seemed to work even when he wasn't fully conscious of our situation.

Just two things worried me. If they couldn't find us, neither could our theoretical rescuers—at least not any time soon. And, though I persisted in telling Vasily otherwise, I thought the biomembranes that were supposed to purify and recycle the air in his suit really might be too old to last until we were picked up—not before poisoning him with the waste from his own metabolism. I took the only precaution at hand, improvising a connection between his suit and mine. Since I don't breathe, my suit's membranes might give him a few more hours of life. But they were probably pretty old too, so unless a miracle materialized soon, my friend was doomed, like he said. As for me—it would be ironic for a pozzie like me to work his ass off to save a human criminal and then end up alone and forced to choose between Chacumbele's inelegant suicide escape and sinking into boredom for the rest of time.

"You know, the more I analyze every move we made, I can't see where we made a mistake, Raymond. It ain't fair. We done everything right, but we never had a chance of winning. All 'cause of that damn Chimera. It oughta be against the law for bad guys to have better weapons than the good guys, don't you think?"

"Whatever you say, Vasily."

"Come on, robot boy. You think I'm such a goner, you gonna say yes to every stupid thing comes outta my mouth? How about you untie me and let me take a walk around that asteroid? Just to take a leak. You know what taking a leak is, I figure, even if you don't have to waste time on such details."

"Sorry, Vasily, I can't. The straps must have gotten damp, nothing perceptible, maybe just a few water molecules per square inch, but that's all it took. The harness knots are frozen solid, and I don't have an anchor point to stand on so I can cut them. If I tried, we'd both spin out of control."

"Hmm. You're sharp, henchman. Sounds logical, almost possible, but I ain't convinced. Raymond, you think I'll make it out of this?"

"As much as I will, Vasily, for sure."

"Not much consolation, but whatever, something's something. Know what? In the holovideos, when the hero's about to die, he always tells the other guy to give his mother this or that, or put flowers on some dude's grave, or tell some girl he wasn't a coward in the face of danger. I got nothing like that to ask you to do for me, and frankly I don't care. When I'm gone—the hell with the world."

"I could always go tell Old Man Slovoban that you gave everything you had trying to avenge him. And give him another suit for his collection. I could tell him that your final thought was for him."

"Ha, that I'd love to see. I doubt they'd let you inside the *Estrella Rom* without me, much less let you get near the Old Man. But I bet you could shoot your way in and give him the suit, if you really wanted to. You'd do that for me, Raymond? Knowing I'd never find out, never thank you for it?"

"You could thank me now, in advance—what do you think? And yes, I'd do it in your memory, if you'd like."

"I don't think you'll get the chance, but thanks all the same."

"Oh, so you don't think they'll find me either, at least not before the Old Man dies of old age?"

"They'll find you, they'll find you. You can sit tight for a thousand years, if that's what it takes. But by then there probably won't be much left of the *Estrella Rom*—see what I mean?"

"Oh. Makrow and Weekman will put two and two together and get Slovoban. But don't you think the Romani defenses can take on the Chimera?"

"Seriously? You think they could?"

"No."

"Good. I was starting to think too many days in space were messing with your judgment."

"Not that many days. It's only been—"

"No! Don't tell me. If you tell me it's been two or three, I'll get depressed. Let me think. We've been out here for a month, or a month and a half, that I'm a hero and our odds of being rescued are going up by the second."

"As you wish, Vasily."

"Raymond, how long has it been since we left the shuttle?"

"Forty-six days."

"An exact number and everything, thanks. How've I done?"

"Great, Vasily. I don't know many people who could have held up for so long without going crazy."

"If I ask you for one more favor, will you do it?"

"Depends."

"Good answer. Raymond. If I start going downhill—not like now, but really downhill, all the time—will you open my air valve?"

" . . . ."

"Please. Or are you guys really bound by Asimov's stupid three laws, so as you can't sit back and let a human die under any circumstances, or what?"

"No. I'll do it, Vasily. But how—"

"Don't worry, you'll know. When I start talking about my mother, my father, and my brothers, that'll be the time. Because I'm an orphan, remember? Promise me?"

"Whatever you say."

"That's what I like, you know, robot? Too bad I hadn't met up with you yet when I was pulling scams on the orbitals. We would have made a good team, don't you think? The human rat and the buratino."

"If you say so, Vasily."

Gaussical or not, he was visibly deteriorating. He was tougher than he looked, but by the end of day ten he was only speaking in incoherent bursts, and only in response to the fragments of Chandler novels I told him. He began getting me mixed up with the characters from *The Big Sleep*, and though I kind of liked being called Philip, it was clear he wasn't going to hold on much longer. The recycling membranes built into the suits were seriously contaminated by his bacterial flora. But at least they were still working, and since we were barely active he wasn't consuming much in the way of nutritional concentrates either.

The worst parts were the silence, the unvarying temperature, the darkness. A human brain needs constant external stimulus or it starts to malfunction. And the time was fast approaching when the sound of my voice inside his helmet would no longer be enough to preserve his mental health—though he still hadn't started talking to his unknown parents. I would have done what I promised, I swear. But I wouldn't have enjoyed it. And he still had moments of lucidity now and then that made me think about things I'd never considered before.

"Raymond, you think Makrow will end up getting rid of Giorgio Weekman himself? He's not worth anything to Makrow outside of this system, and Makrow doesn't seem like the sort of person—the sort of Cetian, I mean—that travels with excess baggage."

"If it's any consolation to you, I think that's exactly what he'll do. I'd been thinking the same thing, Vasily. There's Cetians and Colossaurs all over the galaxy, they say, but as to humans, outside of here—"

"But that poor bastard Giorgio must still believe they're going to take him. I almost feel sorry for him. I would have treated him nicer. A fast, merciful death, no fooling around. But his palsies are likely to jettison him far from nowhere, in some binary system's Oort cloud. Well, at least he'll get to see other suns in the end. I'd like to visit them. Raymond, you ever left the Solar System?"

"No, Vasily. All of us, all the pozzies, are on board the *Burroughs*. In fact, this is the first time I've ever left the station in all my fifty-seven years. And I'd gladly have skipped the trip, now that I think of it."

"Good thing at least one of us still has a sense of humor. But know what, pozzie? I can't say I'm going to die happy. Not if I've never seen the stars, never flown across the galaxy. The aliens always say we're not ready yet, but I say: who are they to decide for us? Who told them they could set themselves up as our lords and gods, with the right to rule over life and death for humanity?"

"Technology."

"Fuck technology. Don't you think we'd be better off now if they'd left us alone? We have heaps of wonderful little gadgets and they might as well've told us they work by magic. Not like they ever taught us how they work or what theories they're based on. We let them turn us into a race of customers. We don't invent anything—what's the point? The aliens already invented more than we could dream up in a thousand years. Get me? I don't think they really even want our raw materials. All they want is to keep us down, keep us like this, neuter our initiative."

"Vasily, that's an interesting intergalactic version of an old conspiracy theory, and I hate to contradict you and tear your theory down—but I know the merchants, and I know that they aren't faking their greed for raw materials, not in the least."

"Raymond, enough shitting around. It's time. Open my fucking valve before I change my mind. Been nice knowing you, really. If I had another life to live I might even think about becoming a cop, if I could have you for a partner."

"Wow, sounds like a declaration of true love."

"Go to hell, bag of bolts."

"We're here already. But changing the subject—you haven't told me about your parents."

"Fuck my parents and my whole family. I want you to open my valve, I'm telling you."

"You're sure?"

"Sure as I'll ever be. Okay, I still remember I'm an orphan, but my mind is going, I can tell. Over your shoulder, I see three stars moving toward us, and stars don't move."

But his mind was perfectly clear. The fact was (thank God—any God, to be on the safe side), those weren't stars.

The three ships from the Milano 5 asteroid prospecting fleet found us on day seventeen of our ordeal, nearly a million miles from the orbit of what had once been Asteroid G 7834 XC. Their hypersensitive instruments succeeded where the Chimera's sensors had failed. Was it once more due to Vasily's strange power, or dumb luck?

No matter. The point is, there they were.

It took the miners ten minutes to decide whether to rescue us after they detected our image. It's easy to imagine the "humanitarian" discussion they had after discovering us: a tranquil, disinterested debate about rewards for rescues, criminal responsibility, and the odds of going to prison, about what would happen if they decided to play dumb and keep going while hushing it all up. . . .

Luckily you can still find a hint of ethics even among asteroid prospectors, that mutant subspecies of space rat. They helped me pull Vasily aboard (his legs, like the rest of his muscles, were no longer responsive after floating in total weightlessness without any exercise for more than two weeks). They grumbled about how he was draining their reserves of blood plasma and fresh food, but they also did their minimal bit to help El Afortunado's debilitated body get back to more or less working order by repeatedly administering general dialysis and intravenous metabolic treatments.

But their protests grew louder and angrier, almost spilling over into mutiny, when I pulled my extraordinary police authorization on them by asking them (by which I mean ordering them) to send us off in one of their three ships to the nearest base where we might catch a rapid spacecraft to the *Burroughs*.

There was shouting, cursing, wailing, and exclamations of "that's what we get for rescuing a damn pozzie alien-hugger" from a couple of crew members. But when one of the prospectors, who evidently invested all his profits in anabolic steroids and nutritional supplements (he wasn't very tall, but his arms were thicker than my thighs and his back was so broad he would only look small next to a Colossaur—so broad that it would be easier to jump over him than to walk around him—and also covered with hair) decided to resort to stronger measures, putting an electric stiletto to my throat when he thought I wasn't looking, I had to show him that the extraordinary powers of the *Burroughs* Space Station Positronic Police Force aren't based solely on rational persuasion and an assumption of good behavior. I'd left all my weapons on the shuttle, but a positronic robot's synthetic muscles don't grow weak after three or even three hundred weeks without exercise and in zero gravity.

After I reduced the rash gorilla's stiletto to a spark-spewing knot and rearranged his overdeveloped right arm into an anatomically dubious angle dangling from his shoulder, his shipmates suddenly became a lot more collaborative.

A lot quieter, too.

That's why I didn't hear until the third day, just a few hours before we landed at the zero-g cubbyhole that the zero-prospect miners called a base, that Vasily had guessed right.

An unidentified ship, coming from an undetermined direction, had attacked the *Estrella Rom* three days earlier, hitting it with so much firepower that all the Romanis' combined defenses were unable to resist after the first volley.

The Chimera destroyer (it could only have been Makrow and his sidekicks, though the bit about the "unidentified ship from an undetermined direction" showed that the aliens were being as hard-nosed about censorship as ever—perhaps for good reason this time; if the human police knew what was orbiting their Earth, they might have refused en masse to man their ships) didn't stop at blasting the whole flimsy structure of the wheel to smithereens. With sadistic thoroughness, they hunted down every wretch, one by one, who hadn't been lucky enough to die in the explosive decompression that blew the shabby station apart when its seals failed. Escape pods and space suits alike became target practice for their sick game of shipwreck hunting. And by all accounts their aim was excellent. The thuggish miner I had beaten described to me, vindictively and with every gory detail, how Earth police were still finding punctured pressure suits and pulverized pods all over the orbit.

Needless to say, no survivors were found.

Vasily was still sleeping and hooked up to at least fifteen tubes when I heard the news. I didn't have the stomach to wake him up and tell him. Old Man Slovoban wasn't Vasily's father, but he was the closest thing to a father the poor guy ever had. Besides, he wasn't going to like it when he found out I had saved him from death in space only to send him back to his cell.

It's true. My superiors had decided that my "Gaussical vs. Gaussical" initiative was a failure. They'd ordered me to return immediately to the *Burroughs* and account for my mistakes.

And, they explicitly added, if I didn't want my situation to get even worse, I'd better come back with Vasily.

NINE

THIS WAS THE MOMENT I'd been dreading all along.

Maybe it was my imagination (after all, only one of the three had what you might call a facial expression), but I saw the Triumvirate of the Galactic Trade Confederation glaring at me from behind their great table like I was a giant turd dumped on their pristine hall.

Maybe a bit more scornfully.

They got right down to business, no greetings or preliminaries.

"Your idea of using a human Psi to capture the criminal Makrow 34 confused us at first. We thought it original, yet it was only suspiciously heterodox and, as was to be expected from such a foolish notion, it ended badly." Scowling in disapproval, Rebbloh 21, the Cetian representative, subtly stressed his Gaussical compatriot's status as a renegade, as if to make it abundantly clear that he and the rest of his species had nothing whatsoever to do with those crimes.

The Cetian's appearance was completely humanoid, his command of Standard Anglo-Hispano impeccable. But neither that nor the fact that he was one of a series of clones hatched from eggs saved him from being an absolute bastard. Good people (if such exist among the Cetians, perhaps as mutants) never reach the top in the Galactic Trade Confederation—or anywhere else in the universe, I fear.

"At least the operation carried out against the asteroid resulted in nothing more noteworthy than human casualties, an insignificant loss compared to the death of one of our own in the first encounter with the criminals," the Grodo representative broke in, interrupting the Cetian (to my great relief). The Grodo's scent-marker name, which obviously has no direct equivalent in spoken languages, meant something roughly like *Lofty Sniffer-Out of Commercial Possibilities That Will Leave His Adversaries Weeping Over Their Empty Coffers*. Fortunately for the translators, he was better known as *Escamita* or *Tiny Scale*, at least among us pozzies. He shifted to a topic he found of far greater importance: his own interests. "The nest of . . . " (here the sophisticated cyberprotein device gave up on translating the dead bounty hunter's pheromonic insectoid name, emitting only a pitiful burbling whistle), "which I represent here, consider themselves mortally aggrieved, but would be willing to forget the offense, given adequate monetary compensation. Considering that the malefactors belong to the Cetian and Colossaurian species, nothing could be more just than to—"

The Cetian forgot his manners and hissed something in his harsh native language, to which the Grodo replied by raising himself menacingly on his hind feet and revealing his long ovipositor sting.

"Please, please!" The hulking armored Colossaurian representative stepped between the rivals. The titanic reptiloid's real name was as unpronounceable as the Grodo's, so he too was instead known by a well-earned nickname: Yougottaproblem. His call for civility made me only more suspicious. One of the most irascible members of the most warlike species in the galaxy, calling for order? There was something fishy going on. "We may speak of compensation later. Colossa is willing to pay any price necessary to put the lamentable behavior of their *representative* behind them," the translation device interpreted him, though I suspect the term the Colossaur used in his own language for the bagger was a good deal saltier. "In the meantime, Makrow 34 and his accomplices remain on the loose, and given their illegal possession of a Chimera-class destroyer they constitute a genuine danger, which is what we must urgently confront."

"They will be hunted down. A single combat ship cannot thwart all the system's police forces, no matter how primitive humans are," Rebbloh 21 objected with an almost human gesture of annoyance.

"A Chimera-class destroyer with a Colossaur at the helm could destroy every base in the Solar System, one by one—except this station, of course—and no human ship could stop it," the Grodo spoke up again, and the Colossaur gave a bow of his powerful head, as if to tacitly thank him for his respectful acceptance of the obviously superior combat abilities of Colossa-designed craft. "I believe that the resolution of this affair has already surpassed the technical abilities of the human race, and even that of the robotic police force on this station."

I almost would have preferred getting chewed out. Being urgently summoned only to be treated like a microbe on the wall wasn't exactly my fondest dream.

"Agreed, it is a major problem. How do you propose to deal with it?" Rebbloh 21 said, making no commitments but clearly sensing something big was up. I sensed it too. "I do not imagine you are thinking of handing so primitive a species the sophisticated combat systems needed to confront this destroyer. The mere presence of which destroyer in this system, incidentally, does not speak well of the supervision of high-risk exports from the Colossa system."

"Those guilty of this criminal negligence have already been punished," Yougottaproblem thundered (and I say *thundered* because there was a sound that the translation device left unchanged, and it sounded precisely like thunder—though more likely it was an especially pungent curse). "This is not however the point." Nothing in the universe can divert a Colossaur from a subject once he's locked onto it. "Considering that we cannot provide advanced military technology to either the humans or the pozzies, and that the tripartite agreement expressly forbids the introduction and operation of military detachments from any of the signatories in our free systems, I propose the creation, for this exceptional case alone, of a task force to capture these criminals and their illegal spacecraft. Pending which, all the commercial operations on this enclave should be suspended and all the independent merchants currently here should return to their systems of origin."

"I support the motion." Escamita reacted on the fly, and if not for the fact that Grodos have no lips, he probably would have smiled. "Indeed, the situation calls for a joint naval blockade so that we can be certain Makrow and his flunkies do not escape from this system in their Chimera."

I almost clapped my hands: it was a masterful move in the old trading game. Which consists above all in breaking your competition. As humanoids, the Cetians were slightly more interested in the raw materials that Earth and the other human colonies of the Solar System could offer them. Indeed, they were humanity's largest trading partner, by a narrow margin. If this proposal for an embargo went into effect, the Cetians' balance of trade could be negatively affected—especially if they were forced to buy the equivalents of terrestrial materials and harvests from planets controlled by Colossaurs or Grodos, as would almost certainly happen.

A dirty trick, but as everybody knows, everything's fair in love and intergalactic trade. Even war, if it comes to that.

"I oppose this measure, and I will exercise my veto power!" Rebbloh 21 responded energetically, immediately grasping the trap they had laid. A Cetian doesn't make it onto the triumvirate of a trading station without first developing an intuition that a Psi would envy for sniffing out traps. A single pirate ship, no matter how powerful, isn't reason enough to freeze all movement in an entire trading enclave. This station closely monitors the only hyperspace portal in the system. If Makrow 34 were crazy enough to attempt an approach, he'd discover that the defenses of the *William S. Burroughs* are strong enough to demolish his ship, powerful as it is, as soon as the radar identified it. . . .

Those last words, *as soon as the radar identified it*, bounced around my mind—and an idea exploded across my circuits: what if it *doesn't* identify the ship?

What if Makrow 34's plan all along was to get us obsessed with the unmistakable outline of a Chimera-class destroyer, while he and his goons slipped through the holes in a net that was only looking for that one vessel?

"I believe that under current circumstances it should be considered utterly inappropriate to exercise the veto power . . . " the Colossaur was beginning to say, a malevolent gleam in his piggish little eyes. But I didn't listen to the rest of the words into which the cybernetic translator converted his bestial grunts and snorts.

I left the three powerful representatives of the Galactic Trade Confederation to squabble over their disagreement and hightailed it out of the room.

Let them work their mess out however they preferred and pin the blame on whoever they wanted. I had more important things to do.

It was like a gambit in chess. If the Cetian Gaussical was prepared to sacrifice his queen (the Chimera-class destroyer), then the pawns (he and the other two bad guys) might make it to the eighth square and get crowned. That would be: the hyperspace portal on the ecliptic plane. If they managed to get out of the Solar System, and especially if they got away with some of their loot, it would probably be a few years before another pair of baggers came within a parsec of them.

Only humans played the game with the sixty-four black-and-white squares. Not even Cetians bothered with it, considering it too simplistic (the closest they had was a three-player game played with sixty variably valued pieces, arranged across five boards of a hundred squares each, placed one above the other to form levels—typical of their mentality; even we pozzies had a hard time following it). But apparently Makrow 34, who had spent a long time running around Homo sapiens territory, had learned it.

But I was good at the old game too. The key to winning at chess is learning how to anticipate your enemy's moves while coming up with unexpected moves of your own at the same time.

I practically flew down the corridor to grab the nearest express elevator. My mind was turning even faster. First off: find Vasily again. He was somehow able to sense Makrow's presence, as he had shown when we neared the asteroid. Or rather, as my friend Einstein would have corrected me, he could detect the altered probability curve that the grotesque Gaussical produced with his Psi powers.

But where should I take him? Which variation on the escape route would the crafty Cetian go for? I had to anticipate his next move if I wanted to lay a trap he couldn't escape.

Of course, they'd have to disguise themselves first: a Cetian, a human, and a Colossaur hanging out together aren't exactly the sort of trio who can stroll past you unnoticed.

Would they also camouflage the Chimera rather than abandon it? Risky, but possible. The destroyer was worth a lot, and they'd have no lack of costume material: according to the rumors on the illegal Web that had reached the mining prospectors, the attack on the *Estrella Rom* had left thousands of bits of debris in orbit, in every shape and size, even whole spacecraft. Maybe they'd even find some tumbledown shuttle with a storage hold big enough to hide a smallish ship like a destroyer.

And why not both variations?

But would they all try getting out together, or would they separate so that at least one of them might have a chance of leaving the system?

Or, as Vasily and I had each thought, maybe the aliens would simply sacrifice their human accomplice as a distraction. Queen sacrifice, pawn sacrifice.

Anything was possible. . . .

Just then alarms began blaring all over the station, and I realized it could only mean one thing: the Grodo and the Colossaur had joined forces to outvote the Cetian, and the *William S. Burroughs* was going to shut down and be evacuated for the first time in fifty-seven years, with all the resulting pandemonium.

An ideal state of confusion for Makrow and his sidekicks to slip away.

I could only wonder if Escamita and Yougottaproblem were also Makrow 34's accomplices.

TEN

"I CAN'T SENSE HIM, I can't see him, I ain't got a fucking clue where he is!" Vasily yelled, and slammed his fist into the control panel, swiveling halfway around to look at me. "Sorry, Raymond. It ain't the same doing it on a holoscreen as live. To start with, if he don't use his powers, I can't pick up on him. Then there's too many aliens, too many humans; he could be any one of them." He buried his face in his hands.

Before him, across the wall of screens, the crowds abandoning our station were heading out in endless, grumbling lines toward the docking modules where their ships awaited, with an orderliness that most often was more apparent than real.

Over there, a bunch of humans were struggling with a number of long, narrow boxes, which must have been filled with very heavy objects considering how they strained to manage their loads, even with the help of antigrav carts.

Here, a Cetian was running to grab the spot left empty by a human being throttled by an angry Colossaur. A crowd formed and the murmuring of the masses rose to a roar until a couple of pozzies arrived and detained the pair.

There, it was a Grodo and another Colossaur exchanging blows. The fight sounded like a hammer striking an anvil, against a choral backdrop of hoarse lions. A space had cleared out several yards wide around the massive opponents, obliging another pair of my buddies to intervene with their anti-riot stun guns (not very effective against such armored monsters, but that's all they had).

It wasn't quite total chaos yet, but it was getting there. As broad as the halls and passages of the *Burroughs* are, they weren't designed for this type of general evacuation, especially not on an emergency basis.

"Oh, don't worry, it was just on the off chance, but we had to try it, right?" I patted Vasily on the shoulder to comfort him, but when I tried to further calm his worries with a joke, I screwed it up badly. "Besides, I'm surprised you're even interested. Seems you weren't so happy in your isolation cell after all, eh?"

He didn't say anything, but the dark look he gave me was worth any number of words. He still hadn't forgiven me for letting him wake up from his zero-gravity ordeal in the same cell where he had spent the previous three years imprisoned. I felt sorry for him, but there was nothing I could have done about it: seventeen days floating in a pressure suit through space might be a subjective eternity, but in terms of his sentence it was just seventeen days. After he'd demonstrated that he could remove the supposedly irremovable anti-Psi collar at will, we couldn't even grant him that sort of conditional freedom—though it's also true that if he hadn't taken the collar off when the Chimera attacked us, neither of us would be around anymore.

So I shut my mouth too, and we kept our eyes fixed on the holoscreens.

He wasn't wearing the collar now, either. He might at least have thanked me for that. But what can you do. Well, he had the excuse that we were too busy.

Once more we were up against the needle-in-a-haystack problem. How can you tell one Colossaur from another? Without his weapons and his gear, the treacherous bounty hunter would be practically indistinguishable in our eyes from any other member of his species. A little bigger at most, but not enough to make a real difference. At night all cats are gray, and at any time all Colossaurs are huge.

As for the Cetians, being clones they're virtually indistinguishable from each other. Anybody not from Tau Ceti would have an impossible time telling the horrific Makrow 34 not only from the harmless Makrow 33 but even from our own dear Rebbloh 21 (who isn't really much better as a person, I suspect). The external differences between Cetians and humans aren't very great either, morphologically speaking—though one species is born from a uterus and the other hatches from an egg. Besides, with costumes and the holocamouflage we have now, details such as their double hearts and the different range of their visual spectrum no longer seem insuperable.

Makrow 34 could be that bearded guy in Module 21 speaking what sounded like Urdu to me, or perhaps Parsi or some more exotic dialect. Or he could be one of the guys struggling with that long, heavy box on the antigrav cart. If Giorgio Weekman climbed onto his shoulders, they'd make a perfect six-member person, just a little ungainly—like that Grodo in Module 9.

The fact was, they could be anybody. When this was over, if it ever would end, I thought, they'd have to think about a system for identifying everybody who enters the station: something faster and harder to falsify than thumbprints, a retinal scan, or even DNA. Cheating their scanners with samples from someone else is child's play even for human criminals, so it wouldn't slow a damned Gaussical at all.

There were too many of them, too few of us, and not enough time to monitor everyone thoroughly. We put a pair of pozzies in every module, but with the continuous flow of evacuees they couldn't check out the crowd one by one. So they picked one person out of every ten—choosing at random, or singling out anyone who seemed suspicious—but even this procedure made the evacuees protest, especially the aliens, who felt their privileges were being violated. Selecting one out of every ten at random was as good as not doing anything at all, given our guy's ability to manipulate the odds.

I was watching several screens at once, trying to catch anything a little off. I knew subconsciously that I was missing something; there had to be at least one clue, perhaps so subtle that my conscious mind couldn't pick up on it. Or was I just carried away by my desire for there to be something, my guilt at not finding anything? I wondered if it wouldn't have been better, more efficient, if the aliens had made us entirely cold, mathematical reasoning machines instead of partly analogic and emotional, subjective, fallible, nearly human.

Maybe we had a slim chance, though. If Makrow lost his nerve and had to use his powers, Vasily could detect it and. . . .

"What really pisses me off," my theoretical fugitive detector exclaimed at last, as if to himself, "ain't that they wouldn't give me my freedom. Say you can't trust me, say you can't be sure I won't use my powers if I'm not wearing the anti-Psi collar, say whatever, and I'll say the same about police promises, including robot police promises: they ain't worth an old fart, far as I ever saw. But that ain't it. What burns my ass is this, we let that slimeball Weekman get away, knowing he'll tell everybody in the galaxy how he pulled another one over on me. And on all you positronic flunkies, too, by the way."

I stopped listening. Something caught my eye on one of the screens. I zoomed in. It wasn't anything out of the ordinary, but . . . instinct? Was I going to start trusting to instinct, too? Module 14. Another false alarm, no doubt. A guy standing behind a couple of humans, who were hauling yet another mysterious long, heavy package (this was suddenly happening all over the station; contraband weapons? Maybe. Under other circumstances I'd have them checked out, but we didn't have time for misdemeanors just then). Hunched, white-robed, with long Rasta locks, sweating, doubling over just before he got to where my buddy Mao Castro stood controlling the line.

The suspicious detail: his skin, which to all appearances should have been black, had gone ash-gray. Why? Stomachache? Scared shitless? I dialed the sound all the way up: yep, the poor guy's stomach was burbling like a pot of boiling water. He vomited; hesitated; tried to stand up straight, rose halfway up, hesitated again, let two or three people pass; then at last he squeezed back into line in front of a Colossaur, who snorted at the insult. Hunched, black, Rastafarian dreads, definitely human, didn't look anything like Weekman or Makrow, though you know that all it takes is the right kind of plastiflesh makeup. . . . But they wouldn't be that crazy, risking the reaction of the ornery oversized Colossaurs, would they? Still, definitely suspicious: if he wasn't one of them, then he was definitely smuggling something. Better call it in. I grabbed the mic.

"Mao Castro: keep an eye on the Rasta in white, he might be . . . " I felt Vasily's breath on my back. "What do you think, Afortunado? Could it be Makrow?"

"No, not him." He hesitated, but he was staring at the image. "Don't look like Weekman, either, but you guys better watch it. Something's off." He leaned forward until his nose almost touched the screen, watching my buddy in his Red Guard uniform approach the suspect. "Huh. Indigestion? Raymond, ever heard of them metabolic bombs, stuff you swallow in your food? The ingredients seem harmless, one at a time, but when your stomach acid breaks them down and they combine—boom! Weekman loved fooling around with rare poisons like that, years ago. Remember what he did to the Old Man. Better tell your Chinese friend to be careful."

"Mao, watch out for the guy in white. Could be a human bomb."

Mao Castro ran toward the suspect and Vasily leaned in closer and closer to the holomonitor, until the inevitable happened: the wheels of his chair slipped forward and he fell clumsily onto his back. I leaned down to help Vasily, as I tried to keep from laughing.

And a thousand suns exploded on the screen.

Holovideo systems are robust and effective, ideal for capturing the three-dimensionality of a scene or a space. But they aren't perfect. Their main disadvantage is, they're too realistic. Or, breaking it down: you can't use optical filters with them, and the light saturation is limitless. That is why they are only used indoors. If a holocamera outside a ship were accidentally to point directly at the sun, the image on the screen would be as blinding as the star itself.

Vasily's Gaussical power—or his good luck—saved us once again. If his chair hadn't had wheels instead of an antigrav suspension, he wouldn't have slipped. If he hadn't fallen, he would still have been watching the screen, and from that close up his retinas would have been permanently burnt. If I hadn't leaned over to help him, the brightness would have overloaded my electro-optical systems—nothing irreversible, in my case; after ten minutes I would have been able to see again—but what if by then it was too late?

Suddenly I realized that it would take any other pozzie monitoring the scene the same ten minutes to return to full operational capacity. I ran to the microphone, imagining the worst. "Mao? Mao Castro?"

Surprise. The screen didn't display the massacre I had feared. Yes, the Module 14 transit hall looked like a wheat field hit by a tornado or a lightning bolt, filled with smoke and bodies lying strewn everywhere, like ears of wheat scattered by the wind.

But setting aside the temporary blindness, they were almost all in one piece, and some were even starting to move again. The number of groans that reached me over the sound channel showed that the wounded greatly outnumbered the dead. Over there was a stunned Colossaur, trying to stand up, tossing aside one of those omnipresent long, narrow, heavy packages, which had landed on him when the explosion hurled it from its antigrav cart. Over here were three humans, trying to stand and tumbling down. Evidently the bomb's power had mainly been used to generate a flash of light.

Even so, the blast was too powerful for the poor people closest to it to survive. I noticed a couple of scattered limbs and a few bloody tatters, implying at least three or four victims. Several bits of cloth were still smoldering, but only a few of them could have belonged to the Rasta in the white robes. Whoever he had been, the explosion must have reduced him to molecules.

As for Mao Castro, I imagined the worst. After all, he had been the closest. And I could see a few suspicious metalo-plastic fragments here and there.

But. . . .

"Raymond, can you hear me?" Though hoarse, faltering, barely recognizable, it was my buddy's voice, and the next second I saw him. Alive, though not exactly whole: missing both legs and one arm, he had managed to drag himself over to the camera and microphone. He was also missing half his face (his shredded black beard was still burning; not a very pleasant scene), but his torso (the only part of a pozzie that really matters, in the end) was relatively intact. It wasn't pleasant to see his damaged thoracic air-compressor voice box pumping through the torn khaki of his mangled Red Guard uniform. It looked kind of like an accordion riddled with holes and kind of like the gills of a fish out of the water, dying.

"I hear you. Are you okay?" I shouted. "I'm going to call for help."

"No, no. . . . Don't call. . . . Must have been . . . diversion. Tell them, go to . . . other modules. . . . Not here . . . not now." And he toppled over, unable to continue.

"Don't worry, Mao. I'll spread the word," I reassured him. "Attention, everyone. There has been an explosion in Module 14. A human bomb. We have a few wounded and two or three dead. Send paramedics and a pozzie repair team. Mao Castro is seriously damaged. Attention! The bomb appears to have been set as a distraction. Redouble the guard in all other modules," I yelled into the communication system. Then I had another thought. "Send a DNA identification team, too. I wouldn't bet on it, but one of the fugitives may have been the human bomb." A second later I had the satisfaction of seeing three people appear in the unmistakable white bioprotection suits of paramedics. At least the aliens have no prejudices in the health field; whatever your race, you can volunteer for the Emergency Public Health and Hygiene Services. "Good." I stood and stretched. "At least the Emergency Services still run like clockwork."

"Good my ass." Vasily's voice startled me, and when I turned around, there he was, right behind me, adjusting the cartridge belt I remembered so well—though I still hadn't seen him use it, or figured out how he'd gotten it from his collection of weaponry and into the control room. But for the moment I had higher priorities than interrogating him on such a minor detail.

"What do you mean?" I asked in all sincerity, ascertaining at a glance that all the weapons in my Gaussical friend's portable arsenal were in their intended holsters. It looked like he'd even acquired a couple new ones. I'd like to know how he got them onto the station, too. Especially because, it occurred to me at the time, if he could do it, it must have been child's play for Makrow and his henchmen. I'd have to expect to find them at least as heavily armed as my friend.

"I think you've lost your detective's nose, Tracy, if you ever had one. You really think it's normal, in the middle of a chaotic evacuation, for a bunch of volunteer paramedics to get to the scene of an explosion in just—" (Vasily glanced at his watch) "—twenty-five seconds?" After checking once more to be sure all his weaponry was where it was supposed to be, he ran to the door.

"You mean . . . you think it's them?" I asked while running to catch up, barely taking time to grab my hat and the highest-power maser I could see in the gun rack. He'd called me Tracy, which meant this was the real deal.

"Who the hell you think they are, Snow White and the Seven Aliens?" he laughed. "I don't know about the other two, but that Makrow—I can feel him. Come on, pozzie. Best decision you ever made coulda been telling your people not to go to Module 14 just yet. That'll give us a chance to have a duel, old-style. Two against three, or if the guy that got blown up was Weekman, which would be almost too good to be true, then two on two." He laughed as we got into the express elevator. "Poor guys, they don't know what a mess they're getting into. Up against Raymond Dick Tracy and Vasily El Afortunado. We should maybe give them a little handicap, like blindfolding ourselves, or letting them fire first, I'm not sure."

I laughed too—but only not to offend him. What I actually thought was that we'd be the ones who'd need a handicap and every other advantage we could grab.

ELEVEN

IT IS BETTER *one hundred guilty persons should escape than that one innocent person should suffer.*

Sounds like a good principle of justice, and really it is—in theory. So much so that most of the time we pozzies try to hold to it. That's probably what Makrow 34 was counting on when he decided to escape through a docking module full of bodies in shock, each of which could make a perfectly good hostage if things went badly for him.

Except that he was the one particular guilty person for whom I was likely to make a big exception. For the Cetian Gaussical I was strangely willing to sacrifice two or three innocents just to be sure he didn't wriggle out again. I'd sacrifice even more if need be. I don't know if I would have gone so far as to invert the saying completely and let a hundred innocents suffer to keep one guilty party from escaping, but I was more than open to an intermediate compromise solution. Say fifty innocents, more or less—more if they were aliens—if it meant trapping these three sons of bitches once and for all.

We had no time to clear out the module or call for reinforcements. Anyway, Vasily didn't want to (neither did I). So we used a simple but effective technique:

We came in running, guns in hand. If the three suspect paramedics reacted, it was them. If not—we'd have to risk a nasty diplomatic incident and oblige them to take off their helmets and submit to DNA scans.

It wasn't necessary. The metabolic bomb guy wasn't Weekman, after all.

It was Weekman who recognized us the instant we stepped out of the elevator. I knew it was Giorgio when I saw him pull an ultrasonic blaster from one of the pockets of his white uniform: he was too small to be the Colossaur, and if he had been Makrow 34 his shot wouldn't have gone so wide of the mark. I get it: he was nervous, oozing adrenaline. Things would have gone better for him if, instead of reacting like a cowboy in an old Western, he'd spent another fraction of a second trying to aim—or more so, if he'd warned his pals before squeezing the trigger.

Even so, the impact of his sonic-wave weapon knocked the hat off my head. But it told me what I needed to know, giving me time to roll aside and dodge the second shot before firing back. Not at Weekman (I wanted to leave him to Vasily—after all, those two had an old score to settle) but at the hulking mass that had to be the Colossaur—unquestionably the most dangerous opponent in an encounter of this nature.

I missed him, firing like a rank beginner. They had realized by then that they'd been discovered, and so I learned that Makrow was now using his powers.

But even the Cetian's abilities had limits. Warding off simultaneous attacks on both of his henchmen was probably pushing it. Evidently he considered the Colossaur more useful in a fight like the one that had just broken out—or rather, I suspect, he allowed Vasily his just revenge on his former human partner, now that Weekman was becoming more of a burden than a help.

In any case, El Afortunado flung himself to the floor and, sliding along it while firing two of his masers without bothering to aim, reached the still unconscious body of a fallen human, which he used as an improvised shield.

Not that he really needed the protection. Whether it was his Gaussical powers or simply his good aim, my partner's first shot tore the visored hood off Weekman's blindingly white bioprotection suit.

With Weekman's head still inside, of course.

I hoped with all my strength it had hurt him. A lot.

Of the three criminals, he was the one I worried about the least. But still: one less. So now things were close to even. Two on two.

Except in the meantime the Colossaur had managed to embed his imposing bulk behind a customs counter, and he was now firing at me from that vantage point with a weapon that no other species would consider a sidearm. The cannon must have weighed over a hundred pounds and measured nearly a foot wide.

I tried to respond with my own comparatively diminutive maser. Powerful as it had looked when I grabbed it, it couldn't do much damage compared to the Colossaur's portable artillery piece. Especially if I couldn't aim straight. Under a constant rain of high-power microwaves, it was risky even to stick my arm out and fire, let alone take time to aim. The first time I tried, the cloth of my precious English trench coat caught fire and I had to turn up my thoracic bellows to blow it out.

By the time his blasts had melted a good portion of the titanium crossbeam I had taken refuge behind, woken up three of the unconscious bombing victims (two of them fainted again when they saw what a hopeless mess they were in; the third, a Grodo, showed a surprising amount of common sense for one of his kind and didn't attempt to join the brawl, scuttering away instead on his six append-ages as fast and as far from there as he could), and set fire to my trench coat three more times, I realized that I was never going to get him like this. If I insisted on continuing to play his game, I'd only be making more victims of those who hadn't scooted out of there yet.

I was like a guy facing off with a slingshot against a tank. In an elementary school playground. During recess.

I analyzed the situation as coolly as I could in the middle of roaring flames. What else should I try? In the old gangster movies, when the good guy finds himself cornered in a warehouse basement or in some cheap hotel, he always leaps out, turns a somersault or two, and runs off with both pistols blazing, saving himself. But I wasn't too sure the Colossaur had watched those movies, so I decided not to try. Most likely he wouldn't know that he was supposed to miss me when he fired his gun, and given the perfect aim he'd shown so far it seemed more like a suicide plan than a solution.

I took a slightly desperate peek at Vasily. The fact that he hadn't washed his hands of the affair, after settling accounts with Giorgio Weekman once and for all, spoke very much in his favor. I decided to thank him—if we ever got out of there.

At the moment, he seemed kind of busy. He and Makrow were trying to part each other's hair with gunfire. But all the time, their own curious Psi powers were at play, and the results were much more spectacular than in my duel with the Colossaur and his microwave cannon.

To start with, they each seemed to be affected by implausibly persistent bad aim. The microwave beams, the lasers, the various classes of projectiles ricocheted all over the place at unbelievable angles, none coming within a few feet of their intended targets.

Now, one stray maser blast did hit the metal counter that the Colossaur was using for cover. The furious roar he let out made it plain that he did not appreciate the heat wave.

A moment later it was my turn for a close shave. A hail of poisoned darts hit within inches of me. The toxin obviously couldn't have harmed my inorganic body, but the closeness of the call told me my position was precarious. Next time it could be something truly destructive, like a thermal tracking missile. I had already noticed that Makrow 34, like Vasily, didn't rely on a single type of weapon. The Cetian Psi was carrying a whole arsenal around with him.

Finally they both decided simultaneously to get smart, shift strategies, and aim anywhere but at their opponent. After this they each had slightly better luck, but only slightly. Gaussical powers to the max. Almost involuntarily I recalled that first Grodo Gaussical fifteen years ago, and I looked around for the two-headed centaurs that some had claimed to see. But fortunately I didn't see anything equine circling us—just one tiny orange Pegasus flitting around in terror, dodging the web of maser and laser fire.

I did notice, however, a whole bunch of other stuff—what my friend Einstein might have called *the collateral effects of a binaural disruption of the probability curve*, something like that. In plain language: the results of a desperate encounter between two Gaussicals using all their powers without restraint. I suppose a physicist could have discovered some very interesting phenomena, such as the multicolored fluorescence around the ceiling, which would have made the brightest aurora borealis seem like a parlor trick. Or the hail that had started falling around us, contrary to all the laws of meteorology and thermodynamics. Or the restless scampering of a troop of little gnome-like creatures that had apparently been asexually reproduced by budding (or by fission; cellular biology was never my strong point) from one of the fallen humans, in Olympic disregard of evolution and its precepts.

As for me, a simple pozzie, I didn't find any of that particularly interesting—much less reassuring. All it did was remind me of the magnitude of the psychic powers at play. And also that Makrow 34's powers were, unfortunately, thought to be much stronger than Vasily's. My human friend wouldn't hold out much longer.

I must admit that even then, except for the occasional microwave beam rebounding a little too close, I didn't feel frightened or even very worried. The situation was deadlocked, true, but that wasn't necessarily a bad thing, at least not for us. We couldn't move from where we were, but neither could they. Time was now on the good guys' side for a change. Vasily and I only had to hold on until the cavalry showed up with the heavy weaponry, all the pozzies in the world. Then it wouldn't matter how many guns Makrow 34 and his stinking Colossaur had, or how formidable and

Gaussical they were; they'd be forced to yield to our superior numbers and firepower.

Unfortunately, they weren't exactly stupid, and they quickly realized that if they didn't escape and right away, they'd never get out at all.

It's funny how time passes when you're under pressure. It felt like I had spent hours playing that game of firing and ducking, but my internal timer reported that we'd been exchanging fire for only three minutes, from the moment we burst into the docking module with guns blazing to the point when the villains were certain that they still had the upper hand and decided to force the situation.

My Colossaur was the first to make a run for it. With an impressive roar, he abandoned his fortress and headed straight at me in tremendous bounds. Imagine a two-ton rhinoceros leaping like a kangaroo. You'd never have expected such agility from his enormous bulk; he must have been buzzed on some exotic class of combat drug. Makrow was quite a fan of such concoctions.

I stole another glance at Vasily and Makrow. The Cetian lowlife must have made the same decision: he had also moved out into the open while firing his guns, which he kept pointed well away from Vasily. But unlike the Colossaur, he moved at his own majestic, leisurely pace, not troubling to run or jump. My friend El Afortunado was doing the same. They both ignored the continual rain of fire each hurled at the other. They looked like a pair of mythical warriors or antagonistic deities confronting one another in a ritual challenge. I saw that they were so focused on the duel, there was no reason for me to expect any danger to come from their direction—or any help, either.

So it was just me and Mama Reptile's supersized son, all alone together.

While he was still bounding toward me, I tried to take advantage of my momentary cover to sharpen my aim. Now that my adversary was out in the open, I should (theoretically) have a better chance of hitting him and, if not knocking him down, at least slowing his charge.

But have you ever tried to hit an enraged rhinoceros that's racing toward you? One that's sentient, war-loving, drugged up the scaly wazoo, leaping like a kangaroo, and firing a portable cannon?

Anyway, I don't think I did too bad. I got him once in a leg and once in a shoulder. But it was like trying to stop a charging tyrannosaurus with a .22.

I could've shot off one of his legs and he wouldn't have noticed. Who knows what sort of drug cocktail Makrow had stuffed into him? As if that weren't bad enough, Colossaur endocrine systems seem to be purposely designed to make them battle to the death. When they fight, their lymph becomes so saturated with endorphins that there have been cases where they have continued rushing forward with enough momentum to crush their enemy's skull between their three-fingered hands even after their own heads have been shot clean off. This case was no exception. The scratches I put on him didn't even throw him off his aim. Quite the contrary, in fact. Or maybe it was Makrow's superior Gaussical powers finally spilling over, even as he concentrated on defeating Vasily.

The weirdest thing was that even while leaping, the elephantine reptiloid had such good aim that he hit me. With that minicannon of his, the logical result was that the blast tore off my entire right arm, almost from the shoulder. Normally this wouldn't have been anything serious—we pozzies don't feel anything you could properly call pain, and of course there was no risk of bleeding out—but wouldn't you know it, that was the hand I had been using to hold my maser.

I watched my weapon sail through the air, still gripped tight by one of my favorite appendages, and found myself disarmed in every sense of the word while my express train of an enemy continued roaring and waving his armored arms and running me down, too close now to need to fire a second shot.

Gulp.

Blessed be the imperfect rationality with which the aliens endowed us. Knowing quite well by a simple comparison of our body masses that I'd already lost our one-on-one before it began, and even being well aware that I'd never be able to grab my maser with my left before being trampled like a daisy under a herd of mammoths, I still insisted on bending down to pick it up.

Had Vasily's powers given me a nudge, or was it merely the absurdity of my action that saved me? The fact is, this time I was the one who caught him by surprise. My naïve mastodon apparently expected me to stand up to him.

One of my attacker's immense lower extremities crashed into my torso, and it was like being swiped by the tail of a titanium dinosaur. I rolled several meters (farther and farther from my maser, by the way) until a wall was kind enough to stop my rolling cold.

It was a steel glass bulkhead. For an instant I saw nothing, then I saw everything black, then blue. Of course, that rainbow was much better that getting hit directly by one of his punches, which would have smashed me absolutely to pieces.

We both began to get back to our feet. I only got halfway up, then stubbornly dragged myself again toward my ripped-off right arm and my gun. What else could I do? He leaped straight back to his feet, getting all inexorable about it, more determined than ever to reduce me to plastimetal pozzie scraps. And as man is the only animal who trips twice over the same stone, he now moved deliberately enough to avoid the risk of slipping or anything so unpleasant as that.

I think I broke the galactic speed record for quadrupeds, but even so I never got within five feet of the trigger. A three-fingered hand the size of a baseball glove closed like a snare around my left ankle, and. . . .

And then it let go. When I turned around, not understanding why he had freed me, I saw that the monster had much more urgent things for his right hand to do than tear me in half.

Such as, for example, helping his left hand keep his own two halves from splitting all along his giant body's axis of symmetry. The reason? Nearly a foot of broad, razor-sharp steel jutting out of his stomach, like it was the most natural thing in the world, right around the spot where a mammal would keep its navel. And all along the straight path that the blade had taken through his tough flesh to reach that spot from the top of his massive skull, the monster was beginning to split into an enormous, fatal V, the edges of which were taking on an exotic turquoise hue.

I couldn't help wondering what that blade was made of. Most likely it only looked like steel and was actually made from a power field or some sort of monomolecular invention. Few known alloys can cut through the osseo-scale armor of a Colossaur.

If I've ever been able to decipher the expression on a Colossaur's reptilian face, it was that day. It was shocked but absolute concentration on the complicated attempt to keep the two cloven halves of his anatomy together—plus his rather fervent hope that if he could do so, the halves would stay together.

For an endless second I too waited anxiously to see what would happen to him—and even hoped in solidarity for him to succeed, when it seemed he might manage the trick. But an instant later, the sword (I had already figured out what kind of weapon it was and was wondering what sort of madman would attack a Colossaur with a simple steel blade—and win) withdrew from the tremendous slash, slipping out gracefully, almost tenderly. The eruption of bluish lymph that was unleashed then sent the titan tumbling.

No living creature, no matter how resilient, can do much after being almost surgically bisected through its brain and spinal cord.

When the giant body fell at length, I finally got a good look at the swordmaster responsible for his defeat—and I admit to feeling shocked. As if emerging from a nightmare about medieval Japan, a thirteen-foot-tall suit of samurai armor was meticulously wiping an interminable blade with a handkerchief, cleaning off its enemy's blue lymph.

It appeared that the blade really was steel, after all.

My eyes were incongruously focused on the twisted expression of sorrowful ferocity on the Japanese warrior's masklike face. It seemed to be saying, "this is going to hurt me more than it hurts you." Not the most reassuring message to be sending. Just in case, I began to reach with my one remaining hand for my gun. . . .

"Shit, that animal nicked my blade," I heard him say, and then I relaxed, though in disbelief. The mysterious samurai was none other than Old Man Slovoban. No one else could have made himself comfortable in armor of those dimensions. I put aside for later the inevitable question of how he'd rescued himself from the massacre of the *Estrella Rom*. "A work by Masamune himself, a dai-katana worth more than its weight in platinum, and to bring it here and mess up the blade like an idiot on the spine of a creature like this . . . " and he kicked the fallen Colossaur with fury. Only then did he seem to notice my presence. He bent down, picked up my detached arm, which still grasped the maser in its hand, and passed it to me with his own hand, long and fine as the claw of a bird of prey despite the armor in which it was encased. "Are you all right, pozzie? You couldn't have thought I'd miss the final showdown with Makrow. I'm sorry I didn't get here earlier. I was so close, in Module 15, but Makrow's and Vasily's powers made things . . . a little difficult for me. That must be what's slowing down your friends now, I suspect. Anyway"—and he kicked the defeated Colossaur again—"one less. I'm afraid we'll never even learn his name. Now we're three against one. Things are looking up, aren't they, buratino? I admit, my idea had been to help El Afortunado first, but since you seemed to be in deeper trouble. . . . Besides, for now the kid looks like he's holding up pretty well, don't you think?" He calmly pointed over his shoulder. "In any case, I don't think it would be easy to get close enough to lend a hand. Honestly, pozzie, don't you notice anything odd?"

I took the hand he offered me and stood up—after first prying back my own fingers (not a very pleasant experience) and retrieving my weapon. The ancient Romani's hand turned out not to be the limp squidlike thing I had expected; on the contrary, it seemed to be pure bone and tendon. I understood then that the samurai suit was not mere armor but a full exoskeleton. Without the help of servomotors, with his jellied bones and almost complete lack of muscles the Old Man would have found it impossible not only to handle a sword as expertly as he had done, but even to walk under gravity.

Makrow and Vasily were still facing off. But now they had abandoned any illusion of taking cover and stood literally face to face. Neither was firing at the other anymore, however. Either they had finally realized that it made no sense to try, regardless of how they aimed, or else they had mutually disabled each other's arsenals with their Psi powers.

I had seen a couple of holovideos of duels between Psis, and what we saw here did look a little like a battle between telepaths. If you squinted, you could also catch a glimpse of the tremendous mental energies at play—something like thin colored veils swirling around the contenders. Psi fields.

It looked to me like Vasily's field was navy blue, almost black, while Makrow's was pinkish white—which for some reason I found almost shocking. Wasn't the purest color supposed to be for the good guy? It's hard to put any credit in archetypes after a surprise like that.

It also reminded me a little of a battle between psycho-kinetics. All sorts of objects were flying around the two rivals: broken boxes, an arm torn off from a victim of the human-bombing, a number of hats (including my own badly damaged fedora). None of it ever so much as touched either of them, though.

But the real, absolute novelty was the *other* thing. And I mean, a genuinely new thing. New to me, to Slovoban, and I imagine to almost every living creature in this universe. After all, it isn't every day that two such statistically rare Psis fight face to face.

Revolving slowly around Makrow and Vasily and spreading out over the veils of their Psi fields, a structure of translucent blades was spreading, widening as the blades grew from the double center where they were being generated. And on those blades. . . .

No. It wasn't anything you'd like to watch. I don't know what sort of effect it had on the hardened old Romani, but as for me, for once in my existence I felt that if I had any hair, it would be standing on end.

Destruction. Crowds of wrathful Grodos scuttling about the *Burroughs* destroying everything in sight. War. A contingent of Colossaurian assault troops disembarking on Earth. Chaos. A hail of missiles annihilating a Cetian ship on approach to the hyperspace portal. Mind-boggling visions of a space station falling to pieces, abandoned, a thousand years in the future. A depopulated Earth. The perfect, cerulean, malevolently inexpressive face of Makrow on a thousand holograms throughout the galaxy. Fierce unfamiliar monsters with insectoidal spikes and mandibles taking over interstellar trade. My own end, torn apart by the claws and mandibles of a kinsman of the criminal Colossaur that Slovoban had just carved in two.

What kind of shit was all that?

A terrible thought came to mind. I didn't know much about the effect of Psi synergy between two dueling Gaussicals (of course, neither did anyone else), but it wasn't written anywhere that it couldn't produce a sort of collateral clairvoyance. So were these visions glimpses of the future? Advance notices of our inexorable defeat and Makrow's victory, in spite of it all?

I hesitated, I admit. For one terrible instant, everything I had been fighting for seemed stripped of meaning and the cold tentacles of defeat and dismay gripped me tight. Nothing but chaos, destruction, war, death? Was there no way out? After all we'd been through? After Slovoban's last-second lifesaving intervention, after he'd kept himself alive through I don't know what miracle?

Then I noticed that, emerging from the whirling blades, between scenes of chaos and death were other images, less distinct: a human delegation touching down on a planet that I knew from its heavy, rough landscape and overwhelming illumination to be Colossa, even though I'd never seen it before; a string of megastations like the *Burroughs* spread across the entire Solar System, all operated and occupied by humans; my own gilded face in a silver holographic frame; the Trade Confederation Council awarding a recognition to Old Man Slovoban, who wore a dress uniform that must have consumed more fabric than the sails of a brigantine.

Perhaps all was not lost yet.

"I know what you're thinking, Raymond." For the first time, the Old Man had called me by my name. "I also think those are possible futures," he said thoughtfully, verbalizing my intuition. "In fact, though I'm no expert in Psi, I'd dare to hypothesize that a Gaussical's power consists in being able to select among them all through some unconscious means, or something of the sort. Take a good look, buratino. If we survive, we'll have been eyewitnesses to one of the most mysterious forces in the galaxy." He lifted his mask, his wizened and misshapen face twisted into a caricature of attentiveness. "But really look. I think things are changing. Maybe Vasily isn't getting the best of it after all. What do you think?"

Silently, I had to agree: judging from the simple proportion between visions of hypothetical bright tomorrows in which we were triumphant and dark ones where Makrow had won, the Cetian was prevailing. In the blades of light, the alternatives in which Vasily, Slovoban, and I managed to muddle through somehow grew progressively smaller and fainter, while there were more and more visions of chaos, death, war, Makrow as emperor of the universe, the end of the Trade Confederation and of life on Earth, the bizarre spiny insect-lizard creatures laying waste to the universe. . . .

"Yes, it looks like Makrow will win after all," I had to admit at last, and it depressed me to do so. But hope dies hard. "If the cavalry doesn't arrive first, of course." Then another terrible certainty began to emerge in my positronic circuits. How had I missed it earlier? If Slovoban had taken so long to get here from as nearby as Module 15, it meant that. . . .

"Well, that's was I wanted to talk to you about. I don't think Vasily can expect help from anyone but us." The Old Man's words fell like a bucket of ice water on the flickering embers of my optimism. "Haven't you figured out yet that something very weird is going on with time? I was less than a hundred yards away when the bomb went off, and I ran straight here with all the strength of my suit. But by my watch, it took me more than two hours to arrive. The funny thing is that I never had the impression that I had slowed my pace at all. And look at these two—"

"You mean they're generating some kind of . . . temporal discontinuity? That's nonsense! Outside of a hyperspace portal, it's theoretically impossible. Time is relativistic," I started to say, quite sure about the small bit of physics I knew. But when I looked where he was pointing, I shut up immediately: not at Makrow 34 and Vasily, but at one of the side entrances to the module's transit hall.

Two survivors of the white-robed human-bomb were just about to leave the module, looking exactly like people who were running as fast as their legs could carry them.

Except that, from my perspective, they were practically motionless; one of them was even suspended impossibly in midair. Only with my acute electronic vision could I perceive that his legs and arms were indeed moving, infinitesimally.

I shouldn't have been surprised—not after seeing the orange Pegasus, the hail, the flying ants, and all the rest, right? But all the same, it simply floored me.

"You're right. This is a time acceleration zone. Time is passing at least ten thousand times faster than normal, and those two are the epicenter," I heard myself say, in the pedantic, neutral tone I've always hated. "Remarkable. Very interesting."

"Maybe, for a physicist. For us, and especially for Vasily, it's terrible." Looking at me sidelong, Old Man Slovoban again unsheathed his long sword and lowered the fierce Japanese war mask over his already masklike face. "Okay, buratino, what are you planning to do? This means that if we don't help him ourselves . . . " His voice was distorted by the metal sounding board inside the mask. "I still think we most likely have a bit of a chance, though. There's a possible future which, from what I can tell, neither of them has taken into consideration."

It took me nearly a second, but at last I understood what he was talking about.

Wow.

But I didn't reply. There was no need.

All right, it seemed we had no choice. Everything for the good guys to win. To be on the winning side, even if we wouldn't be around to enjoy it.

I wondered if Old Man Slovoban was also a chess player. Probably. . . .

I drew my maser, checked the charge level, examined the few half-melted joints remaining in the shoulder of my detached right arm—all the little delaying maneuvers one does before facing up to the only possible course of action.

And then, together, with a savage war cry, the Romani and I went after Makrow 34.

TWELVE

I'M TELLING THE STORY, so it doesn't take a genius to figure out that it all turned out okay, right?

But don't expect me to tell you exactly how it happened.

All I can say is that Slovoban and I ran full speed into the aurora. We both did what had to be done, and there was a bright flash of light, and another, and another, and then—a great darkness.

The next thing I remember are the faces of Sandokan Mompracem and Einstein leaning over me. "Good, he seems to be recovering; shouldn't be any lasting brain damage." The image I had of them was pretty blurry, and I realized that I was looking at them through a single eye.

It turned out, not only was my other eye missing along with nearly half my head, but also one leg from the hip down, and the foot and part of the calf of the other. All destroyed by a series of blasts from my own maser (my colleagues couldn't understand that part), still gripped tight by my left hand, which had been welded nearly shut.

I had suffered inexplicably few wounds to my torso, though. My cerebral computer was returning to full capacity. The peculiar blackout I'd suffered—the first time any such thing had happened to a pozzie—had been caused by some sort of temporary sensory overload from my constant adjustments to the shifting realities generated by the two Gaussicals. Or so Einstein theorized—and who was I, barely an eyewitness, to contradict an astrophysics expert?

While my buddies were picking me up with care so that I didn't fall apart completely, I looked down and saw, to my great satisfaction, that Makrow 34 would never again be a problem for Vasily, for me, for the Galactic Trade Confederation, or for anyone else.

A good twelve inches of dai-katana jutted from his left eye socket like an impossible steel pupil. His right eye was opened ridiculously wide, forever frozen along with the rest of his face in a curious, almost human expression of surprise. As if he couldn't understand how such a thing had happened.

Good for the Old Man. At last he'd had his revenge.

A couple of Grodo volunteers from Public Health and Hygiene (real volunteers this time, not wolves in sheep's clothing), also looking like they didn't understand what had happened, were covering the Cetian's body with a white blanket, preparing to cart it off on an antigrav stretcher.

Another pair of volunteers, Colossaurs this time, were huffing and puffing under the apparently immense weight of another stretcher, long and with no antigrav system. Bouncing and sticking out from under this white blanket were a pair of feet and a long stretch of leg. On top of the sheet lay a tray, from which a very familiar Japanese war mask jeered at me for the last time.

I turned around to ask Einstein about it, but he cut me off. "Don't even try. Your thoracic compressor was the only part of your torso that got torn apart. I'm sorry, but that was Old Man Slovoban's last battle—at least he fought well to the end. His . . . assistants have already been captured. Actually, most of them turned themselves in, and none offered much resistance. That was how we learned how he managed to escape the attack on the *Estrella Rom*: he had time to get himself into the suit of armor he was wearing." He pointed at the long figure that the Colossaurs were just then carrying out the door. "Not only did the suit have enough servomotors to move an army, it was also a fully functioning space suit. He must have hidden out among the debris from the station and evaded the Chimera's sensors. Later, his flunkies smuggled him aboard here, armor and all, in one of those long, narrow, heavy boxes. There were lots of them around today, didn't you notice?"

Of course: heavy boxes, ten feet long. That was the detail I'd been missing. How hadn't I seen it earlier? In front of my eyes the whole time.

Well, it didn't matter now. All's well that ends well.

But had it really ended well? What about Vasily?

"Vaaa . . ." I managed to half croak and half stammer.

"No worries, your human friend is fine." This time it was Sandokan Mompracem who cut me off. "Totally exhausted, is all. Confronting Makrow was too much for his powers. He spent all his neural reserves and collapsed from the stress. But what a pity about the old gypsy. A genuine warrior. He's been the hero of the day. Too bad there's nothing to see but blurs on the holotapes. I'd love to watch him split that Colossaur in two, see how he did it. What I'll never understand, though, is why he decided to cut off his own head."

"I wish I could see how he did it, too," Einstein added. "It's incredible how he arranged it so that, when his sword fell, the blade bounced off the floor in the craziest way—imagine, bouncing up and stabbing Makrow straight through the back of the head! So weird. I'd say it was the most bizarre coincidence ever, except that with Gaussicals around there's no such thing as a coincidence. I suppose Vasily must have called on his last reserves of strength when he saw his father figure die. Never underestimate the power of revenge for living creatures, right, Raymond? No, don't try to talk."

I didn't say anything, didn't even nod, though I easily could have. I only smiled.

Coincidence? Of course. A well-controlled coincidence.

Slovoban had hit the nail on the head. A future that neither Makrow nor Vasily had foreseen, a chess move that neither of the two great egotists expected.

A sacrifice. But not the queen sacrifice that Makrow had attempted by abandoning the Chimera; a total sacrifice. King sacrifice. A king to be avenged.

It was a matter of reflexes; I went first. One leg, then the other, finally a shot to my own head. I could have ended it all quickly just by shooting myself in the torso, but I didn't. I'll never know why. That's the downside of not being a creature of logic. Was it from fear of ceasing to exist, what humans call the instinct for self-preservation, or was it to give Vasily more time to understand our plan?

Who could say? And who would care?

The main thing was that when Slovoban sacrificed himself, El Afortunado already had gotten the whole picture; he was alert, ready to make maximum use of that unforeseeable, extraordinary, foolish act, which introduced a new variable in the equation of the thousand possible futures that had been at play, the equation in which Makrow 34 had been beating him.

The Cetian, for his part, didn't expect it at all. Perhaps because suicide is so extreme among living creatures that it's not the sort of act anyone usually imitates just because they see it done—especially not a mere second later.

Coincidence or symbolism? I guess the almost impossible bounce of a dai-katana forged by the almost mythical

Japanese swordsmith Masamune served Vasily's purposes as well for the occasion as a twin pair of meteors would have if they had sliced through all the shields of the *Burroughs* and pierced both of the Cetian's twin hearts at once. The fact that the sword blow was much more symbolic doesn't count for much when there are so many probabilities at play.

I don't think he even had time to choose.

THIRTEEN

VASILY RECOVERED from his exhaustion and stress after a couple of days. Then, surprise of surprises, the aliens awarded him a supreme honor, one no human had ever been given before. In addition to granting him the practical equivalent of conditional freedom, they invited him to visit the Grodo home world, no less.

Well, *invited* is a polite way of putting it.

To be more precise: they *ordered* him.

Actually, every alien who knew anything at all about Psi was very interested in the curious form of synergy manifested in his probabilistic duel with Makrow 34. So the Cetian and Colossaurian scientists also "extended their invitations." But Escamita's people were able to push the fact that *Lofty Sniffer-Out of Commercial Possibilities That Will*

Leave His Adversaries Weeping Over Their Empty Coffers had
been the victim of criminals from the other two species. In
other words: all three species of aliens trying to screw each
other over, as usual.

In short, life on board the *Burroughs* seemed to be returning to its normal rhythms.

With a few notable changes. For example, the Grodos
insisted on having Einstein accompany Vasily to their
planet. Not exactly as a bodyguard, either.

Who said an artificial intelligence can't feel genuine scientific curiosity? My buddy seemed to have devoted himself
wholly to physics and related sciences.

After a couple of conversations with me, in which he was
skeptical of the temporal chaos I told him about, Einstein
finally had the (brilliant!) idea of replaying the Module
14 holotapes at ultra-slow speed, slowed by a factor of ten
thousand. That was what it took to make the scene of our
double sacrifice, Slovoban's and mine, entirely visible, and to
convince Einstein that no tricks were involved. The clashing
powers of two Gaussicals could produce the same time dila-
tion effect generated by transit through a hyperspace portal.

I admit, I didn't get much out of his enthusiastic expla-
nation—but it seems that the Grodos did. A little of it got
through to me, though:

Broadly speaking, it seems that there had been a couple
of important empty boxes in the general framework of Psi
phenomena. Among all the races of the galaxy, no beings

capable of teleportation or of foreseeing the future had been found.

But the probabilistic duel between Makrow and Vasily had led first Einstein and then the alien specialists to hypothesize that perhaps there was a way (rather twisted, but a way after all) to get around the Law of Causality and catch a little glimpse of the future.

And my friend might be the key to that way.

So: almost a happy ending, at least for him and Einstein.

In any case, nothing could alter the fact that they will be, respectively, the first Homo sapiens and the first positronic robot to pass through a hyperportal and leave the Solar System. I hope all goes well for them.

In other words, I hope that they can both return (someday), that my buddy doesn't get dismantled, that instead he gets his secondname (I suppose he'll pick Bohr or Newton or some such), and that El Afortunado gets treated better than the average guinea pig.

The last time I saw him was at the ceremony where we scattered Old Man Slovoban's ashes. Not in orbit around his beloved planet Earth, as the indomitable Romani probably would have preferred, but out of a hatch on the *Burroughs*. But something's something, isn't it?

El Afortunado was wearing a space suit and I wasn't, so naturally we didn't speak. Nor did we say goodbye. Maybe it was better that way. Man-to-man conversations, or even man-to-positronic robot, are never easy. I know we had a lot of things to say to each other—and I also know that neither of us would have known how to start.

The formidable Chimera destroyer was found orbiting Neptune's moon Triton—with only a handful of energy crystals on board. The rest of the fabled trove? A mystery. The Treasure of Makrow 34 will probably turn into one of any number of myths about the Solar System.

As Slovoban had guessed, the government of Colossa never deigned to reveal the name of their wayward behemoth. A curious sense of honor, to say the least. Something like "he was a fucking traitor, but he was our fucking traitor."

As for me, "in recognition of my outstanding service," the aliens put a little pressure on my buddies to grant me nothing less than the privilege of a secondname.

I think I surprised everybody with my choice.

Oh, I suppose they all expected me to pick Chandler. Sure. But I figured that would be like naming a dog Dog. Too commonplace.

Hammett, Spillane, Himes, or even Tracy (after old Dick) would also have been on the list of unsurprising choices for those who knew me. I imagine more than one might have bet on Fernández as a logical pick—after all, without Vasily and his powers, Makrow 34 would still be a thorn in everyone's side, and I'd still be just plain Raymond.

But Slovoban? Nobody saw that coming. An old gypsy mafioso I'd only met twice? (Though the second time around he did save my life, of course.) A heroic death, but a suicide, after all.

I hope Vasily finds out what I did someday, out there among the Grodos. He left before I was given the honor.

Some have told me that this story shouldn't get filed away in a bureaucratic report. They say I should write it all down, in words, old style, the way Chandler would have done it. The original Raymond.

And maybe I will. Someday.

If I do, I'd like to begin this way:

The desert wind was blowing that night, loaded up on red dust. . . .

ROME, OCTOBER 23, 2002

ABOUT THE AUTHOR

Born José Miguel Sánchez Gómez, YOSS assumed his pen name in 1988, when he won the Premio David in the science fiction category for *Timshel*. Together with his peculiar pseudonym, the author's aesthetic of an impenitent rocker has allowed him to stand out among his fellow Cuban writers. Earning a degree in Biology in 1991, he went on to graduate from the first ever course on narrative techniques at the Onelio Jorge Cardoso Center of Literary Training, in the year 1999. Today, Yoss writes both realistic and science fiction works. Alongside these novels, the author produces essays, reviews, and compilations, and actively promotes the Cuban science fiction literary workshops Espiral and Espacio Abierto. His novels in English include *A Planet for Rent*, *Super Extra Grande*, *Condomnauts*, and *Red Dust*, all translated by David Frye.

ABOUT THE TRANSLATOR

When he isn't translating, DAVID FRYE teaches Latin American culture and society at the University of Michigan. Translations include *First New Chronicle* and *Good Government* by Guaman Poma de Ayala (Peru, 1615); *The Mangy Parrot* by José Joaquín Fernández de Lizardi (Mexico, 1816), for which he received a National Endowment for the Arts Fellowship; *Writing across Cultures: Narrative Transculturation* in Latin America by Ángel Rama (Uruguay, 1982); and several Cuban and Spanish novels and poems.

RESTLESS BOOKS is an independent, nonprofit publisher devoted to championing essential voices from around the world, whose stories speak to us across linguistic and cultural borders. We seek extraordinary international literature that feeds our restlessness: our hunger for new perspectives, passion for other cultures and languages, and eagerness to explore beyond the confines of the familiar. Our books—fiction, narrative nonfiction, journalism, memoirs, travel writing, and young people's literature—offer readers an expanded understanding of a changing world.

Visit us at restlessbooks.org